Love,
Darlene Navor
2016

NEIGHBOR to the AMISH

By Darlene Navor

authorHOUSE®

AuthorHouse™
1663 Liberty Drive
Bloomington, IN 47403
www.authorhouse.com
Phone: 1-800-839-8640

First published by AuthorHouse 7/23/2010

ISBN: 978-1-4520-4491-0 (e)
ISBN: 978-1-4520-4490-3 (sc)
ISBN: 978-1-4520-4492-7 (hc)

Library of Congress Control Number: 2010910035

Reference: 800PaDutch.com

Printed in the United States of America
Bloomington, Indiana

This book is printed on acid-free paper.

TABLE of CONTENTS

INTRODUCTION:

Vaguely knowing about the Amish culture, I just thought they were similar to the Pennsylvania Dutch. My great-great-grandmother on my mom's side was a Dutch Quaker originally from Pennsylvania, hence my Dutch portion of my ethnic heritage. I was told she made quilts. I have the greatest respect for these people since they are practical, humble, and thankful folks, and perhaps somewhat naïve. Nonetheless, I had an overwhelming curiosity about knowing more.

I knew the Amish live without any plug in appliances or gadgets in that they rely on no electricity, therefore no lights to switch on, no refrigerator/freezers to keep food cold/frozen and no telephone in their homes. There are no electric sewing machines, rather, ones with peddles to pump. They sew and make their own clothes and they wear no name brand clothes like what we buy.

Absolutely, there are no cars for transportation, yet. To go places locally, they count on their horse and buggy drawn carriages every season of the year including winter. They may call upon certain willing regular citizens of the community to take them to town or the local general store.

They may need to shop out-of-town for bigger or bulk merchandise, visit local Amish folk, or make longer, out-of-state trips to visit with their Amish relatives or go to funerals.

I know you may have many questions in your mind about the Amish community, and like myself want to learn more. Perhaps, you chose my story for pleasure reading. Along the way, I will talk about dentistry, the general store, herbal treatments, schooling, church, dress, gardening, cooking, social functions, duties for various family members, and livelihoods, etc. of the Amish. As I weave this tapestry or tell my story, I am learning first hand knowledge about this culture and will share with you.

CURIOUS to KNOW THEM

When I was teaching reading to at risk primary graders in California, a fellow teacher had mentioned she went back East for her summer vacation. She and her family stopped in Wisconsin or Minnesota to do an Amish Tour. I think it may have been the very same tour that is available here locally. She was in awe about how every child had chores like boys gathering loose branches and going about their business so diligently and humbly. They were so polite to the tourists and common folk like us. They are indeed. I will go into detail later on in my story about chores.

Knowing the Amish lived around the bend when I moved to Minnesota with Ray in February, 2001, I was eager to learn more. It was a deep thought of mine that stirred me on at least once a month. Ray said that the Amish live just down the hill and around. I thought he meant miles away. He meant it literally. How neat! Every time we would pass by and see children and/or their mothers in the front yard, we would wave and they would wave back with a complacent smile, although, not overexcited. I always had a curiosity about their way of life, because I came from humble beginnings as well.

TIME to REDO the ROOF

Ray called upon our Amish neighbor to redo the roof of our house in May of 2001. Of course, he went to talk to Richard who lived down the hill from us. He has a construction business in the Amish community and hires his fellow Amish neighbors to built houses, barns, and buildings and such for the local country community. They do not do any construction or work in town or city. Before they started ripping the old roof off, I had the pleasure of meeting our neighbor, Richard. He instructed his three or four workers, and had to go on to another job site in the area. He has a driver to take him here and there. During the course of things, one day I kindly asked one of the workers when he was down on the ground, if I could take a picture of them working.

He paused for several seconds and said, "Oh sure, as long as they don't know..."

I said, "I just want to do the right thing. Thank you."

"Thank you, " I said, again, appreciatively.

I went into the south yard about one hundred feet to get a good view of the three on the roof and clicked a couple pictures. I guess one more snapshot wouldn't hurt. I had to capture the moment, but I thought it would be proper to ask first. They, ultimately did a great job roofing the black shingles on our white house. The snow melts or absorbs faster on a black surface.

The Amish started on our addition in November, 2004, after we had a local company dig and lay concrete so we could extend our basement.

Richard, got together a five to six "man" crew which included a fifteen and nineteen year old, their father, and uncle. One can imagine how the young men learn a construction trade. They learn from their older family and friends. It took all half dozen of them to get the floor on. Winter set in so they had to stop building. We covered the floor/basement ceiling with a giant tarp and weighed it down with rocks and bricks for a couple of months until Richard and his crew could start again.

The harsh winter let up and the working crew returned. The framing for the walls took the strength of the half dozen crew all day. They would come every morning with their horse and buggy and tools. No electrical tools, but battery charged drills were allowed. They halted for one hour for lunch and rest time. I felt it was my duty to offer drinks like a can of lemonade, orange soda, coke, or seven up. They did not choose to drink coke, so I knew, then, they prefer not to have any drinks with caffeine. They always thanked me for anything I gave them whether it was the chocolate chip cookies or egg rolls I made. I knew they always brought their lunch in a playmate type cooler. Still, I love to feed!

The crew worked on the addition and remodeling practically day after day. If it was raining, they could do work inside, or if something needed to be finished outside before getting to the inside, they would work half a day on another construction site. There were and are always other homes and barns to be built of steel construction nowadays. They, ultimately, completed the new, white vinyl siding on our addition of a larger washroom, and three bedrooms. Plus, they tore off the old, weathered wood siding from the other half of the house and installed new, white vinyl siding there. We had our brand new addition finished by March 2004.

Ray told them to leave the back porch and front porch for him to finish siding. He did get it done before summer's end.

MEETING ALL the FAMILY

I had it in my mind's eye, I was going to meet the Amish someday. That day came to fruition.

It was a warm Sunday afternoon when I was working in the garden on a mid summer day in 2005. I saw what looked like James and his mom walking up the road toward our house since I had not met Thomas or the older sister, Sofie, yet. In our conversation, I learned that they go for long walks around the country side on Sundays, so they said. I gave them some tomatoes and zucchini from my garden. It was great to finally meet some of the family for starters.

Eventually, Sofie came over on a flat bed horse drawn wagon loaded with a couple of bushels of apples that she already picked, with permission, off the neighbor farmer's trees. Seeing her coming up the driveway... Ray and I were already outside when she got down and approached us.

"Do you have any apple trees to pick?"

"No, but we have some plums that are ripe and you can pick them, I replied."

I gave her two little brothers who rode over with her an ice cream bucket each to put the plums in and she used the outer layer of her dress to hold them until I got a grocery bag for her. I expressed how I always wanted to learn how to jar or "can." I never lived close to my grandmother to learn. My mom certainly didn't can, so I never had the opportunity.

She and her mom planned to make applesauce the next morning, so she invited me to come over tomorrow (Saturday) about 9 AM to watch or learn how to jar applesauce. What an opportunity to meet the Amish family neighbors! I think I arrived the next morning at about 9:15 AM, and they were already done. (I, perhaps, was not aware of their time variance of an hour). I first met Kitty, the mom. She gave me a jar of applesauce to try. The dad was apparently outside and about working the farm. They have cattle and horses. I didn't meet him that day.

All in all, there are thirteen children - eleven boys and two girls - ranging from twenty-one years down to three years. They all (except for the three oldest boys who were out and about working) stood in a group with some in the front and some in the back as Kitty stated their names, ages or grades in school.

I sat at kitchen table and told her how much I love children and since I was a teacher, would love to give them some art lessons. I gave the kids some crayons and paper. Clay was interested since he was not going to school anymore. (When the children complete the eighth grade, they are finished with their academic education and, then, learn a trade or craft.) He went to work building log cabins at a nearby Amish farm. I never ended up giving him those lessons.

THE GENERAL STORE

I think, it was Theo who came over one day and asked if I had time to drive his mom to the general store to get groceries.

I responded, "What time does she need to go? I can be there in half an hour or so."

"That will be fine," he said.

So I picked up Kitty and she was ready with her long, navy blue dress, bonnet, and handbag. We spoke little, as she admitted to not saying much. Only when we arrived at the general store, she said,

"Do you want to come in and look?"

"Oh, I guess I'll look around?" I got out of my car after she was already going in the door to the store."

I found that the store had all the basic non to semi perishable food items like five to ten pound bags of flour, sugar, boxes of cereal (generic brands), packages of chocolate chip, oatmeal, and sugar cookies, gelatin dessert and tapioca pudding mixes, dry lentils, generic brand facial tissues, and cans of vegetables and beans. One will not find coffee or coke here at the Amish general store.

There were reams of fabric in teal, aqua blue and navy blues, green tones, dark browns, white and crème colors, spools of thread, kitchen utensils such as spoons, knives, and forks, rugs in similar colors as the fabric, baby clothes, men's pants and some shoes, women's handmade aprons, towels, potholders, children's books published for the Amish community, socks for everyone, and circular, wall thermometers with deer or bird designs, etc. Other gift items are items carved out of wood like frames, pencil holders, decorated chimes, key chains and calendars.

When I brought Kitty back to her home, I helped her unload the bags and boxes of stuff, some into the house, and some on the grass.

"How much do I owe you?" she inquired.

"Oh, nothing, nothing," I modestly told her.

She, then, came out with a loaf of bread as payment. I believe, the next time I drove her, I got brave and asked two dollars for the gas only. Then, it became a flat three to four dollars a trip, especially when I drove her into town and around a few stops. Yes, I usually stayed in my car as a rule. I only went in the stores if I needed to buy groceries or deposit in the bank as well. Sure, I don't make it obvious, even it is understood that someone drives the Amish into town and is totally acceptable.

I, also, drove Sofie, by herself, to the general store one day to get groceries and fabric or material, so she could sew a winter coat for herself. We stopped at a friend seamstress's house. I guess, she wanted to visit and get some sewing tips. Yes, I am sitting in my car reading a book. After about half an hour, she expressed wanting to go to the Amish flower nursery. Now this is up my alley! I had to go feast my eyes on the pretty, colorful yellow & black pansies, fuchsia, purple and white petunias, tomato, bell pepper seedlings and other plants since it was indeed planting season. Of course, I bought some of those colorful petunias. I planted them outside by our kitchen window and they lasted through the summer until first of October.

She introduced me to her brother James's fiancé at the flower nursery. It made me feel good to know her. (James is the young twenty year old who help build our addition last year.) She is twenty-nine years old. I think James once told me his sweetheart was older than he. No problem.

We were almost to her house, when she wanted to go see some friends on another road southward, but it was getting dark. She decidedly said she would go another time. I would think her mom didn't want her to be out after dark. Sofie was twenty-one years old and was considered to be on her own, even though she still lived at home.

VISIT to the DENTIST or
IN SEARCH OF...

Sofie needed me to drive her to her Amish relative/cousin to have her molar pulled. Now I thought she told me that she had dentures, so I thought that was for all her teeth. If her molar was hurting her and "needed to be pulled," then her lower teeth, I assumed, were real.

Off we went, to her relative-dentist's house about four miles from here. We arrived.

Sitting in the car waiting for thirty-five minutes, she finally came out. I'm thinking, she already had her tooth pulled.

"How did it go? Are you okay?" I empathetically asked.

"Oh, I didn't get the tooth pulled, yet. We need to go where he is working. He is tearing down a barn. The people who bought the house do not want the barn in their back yard...I was just talking to his wife...She said that they need a teacher to teach school here," Sofie continued.

Anyway, she didn't get her tooth pulled, yet...

We had to go track him down where he was tearing down a barn. She directed me where that was. We found him on the roof with what looked like a tire iron tool, prying or loosening some metal sheets away from the barn side. That reminded me of what a dentist might do. They both came back to my car. She got in the front and he, in the back seat.

I greeted him, "Hi! How are you?"

"Oh fine, just working." he said, catching his breath.

11

I drove them back to his home and again patiently waited in the car for forty-five minutes, while Sofie got her tooth pulled. I was reading my book, but I decided to pause and call Ray on my cell phone.

"I'm still here," I told Ray. I quickly explained our go around adventure.

"Why don't they invite you in?" Ray inquisitively inquired.

"That's okay. I just wanted to let you know how it's going. I love you."

Alas, Sofie and her cousin dentist came out of the house. They boarded the car and I drove him back to work. Sofie got out to go talk to a young man who was helping the dentist tear down the barn. She came to the car about half an hour later.

"I'm sorry, you know me. I had to talk to a friend.... " she explained.

"Don't worry, that's ok."

We called it a day. She gave me three dollars for gas.

THE "PRINT SHOP"

Sofie came over to see if I could take her to town to the "print shop." She needed to duplicate some of her designs/lessons for her students that she was going to teach.

"If only you had told me earlier. I could have copies some of them for you," I said kindly.

"Oh, can you…?" she asked with a marveled facial expression.

"I will bring you back to my house and I can copy a few for you. It's the ink that cost, I explained. Let's go into town first and see if they can make some copies. I need half an hour to get ready and then I will pick you up."

She rode back home on her pony.

Shortly, I picked her up and drove her into town. I later realized it wasn't a print shop, per say. Before we passed the newspaper office, I told her that she was going to have to direct me which way the "print shop" was?

"There it is!" It was the PRESS where the local newspaper is printed once a week. Parked on the main street, I waited for her sitting in my car for about forty minutes. She is finally done printing or making what she said was black and white copies of her "lessons" that she was going to distribute to the children in her class.

Before I took her home, I brought her to my house, since I said that I would help her make colored copies. I copied so many of one design and so many of another four designs. I charged her about seven dollars.

THE DENIM DRESS

One day when Sofie came over to call the country lady she had been cleaning house for. I was within hearing distance, and did not intend to eaves drop. She told her that she got a job teaching the Amish children in Wisconsin and could no longer work for this lady.

I decided to give her a short sleeved denim dress that I no longer wore as it was just hanging in the closet.

"Here, could you wear this dress? I don't wear it anymore, so I think you could use it. Can you wear it under your other clothes or around the house? I asked.

"Oh no, we can't use it, but we can make something out of it," she explained.

"Okay," I was assured. I knew she would put the material to good use. I visualized it being cut up to make a quilt if anything.

As we talked briefly, Sofie told me they needed a teacher to teach sixteen, or so, young primary grade Amish children of mostly girls near a real small town in northeast Wisconsin. It was a brand new schoolhouse. They were going to pay her forty-five dollars a day, instead of fifteen dollars a day teaching school for the Amish here locally. Anyway, she accepted the job in Wisconsin. Funny, she told me a year ago that she never wanted to be a teacher. That's when I, again, told her that I was a teacher and wouldn't mind teaching art and reading to the Amish children. (but for fifteen dollars a day, I now learned.)

I, later, learned from Thomas that she had already had left in mid September to teach the youngsters in Wisconsin and was enjoying it.

AGREEMENT to CARE
for the ANIMALS

In August, 2006, Thomas agreed verbally to take care of the twelve sheep, five Emus, and three cats while we were gone to California in mid September for eight days. Since Thomas did feed and water the animals back in April, 2006 for a week, we thought we would ask him again. Guess what? Thomas forgot to feed and water the animals while we went on vacation for a week to California. We thought, he knew the routine as Ray showed him the rounds with the sheep, emus, and our three cats.

I found out when I went to deliver a message that Sofie had called to want to speak to her Mom on the telephone. (I noticed Kitty was sewing by the light of the window what looked like something like a child's jacket from the denim dress that I gave Sofie.)

She said, "How much do I owe you to deliver the message."

I said, "Nothing, nothing, only when you use the phone." I told her to tell Thomas "Thanks!" for feeding the animals while we were gone.

She interjected, "I don't think he went over to feed the animals."

I was shocked, then disappointed, especially when I saw Thomas on my way out. He told me, he forgot to feed the animals because they were busy pulling the corn.

I was mad for over a week and a half. I didn't think Thomas would have the nerve to come ask to use the phone. I professed to myself and

Ray agreed with me. We couldn't rely on Thomas to feed the animals if we ever left the farm again.

FORGIVENESS

The shooting of several young Amish girls in Lancaster County, Pennsylvania had just happened and was blasted all over the news.

I didn't think Thomas would have the nerve to come ask to use the phone, but he came around. He said that their Amish community does forgive this man that committed such a horrible crime. God knows the girls will go to heaven, but that man won't.

I said, " Yes, we have to forgive when someone does wrong and a weight came off my shoulders just as I said it, thinking of his forgetting to feed and water the animals when he said he would.

Thomas came over to use the phone to call his sister, Sofie, who was staying with her Amish aunt whose community allowed her to have a phone in their home. I don't know if it was cellular or landline. Anyway, I brought the Amish School mishap to his attention on the evening news and ask if he wanted to or is allowed to see TV. He wanted to, so he hung up with Sofie and came in the kitchen to view it. After eight minutes, he said that he had to go and couldn't see anymore.

SUNDAY MATINEE

Thomas, Theo, and Clay came over to use the phone to call their sister, Sofie.

Thomas said, "She's homesick."

I said, "Oh, did she call?. They said, "No, but we heard it from others."

Thomas called his sister and talked for a while. The phone was handed to Clay, then Theo.

Thomas and Clay wanted to see a western movie. They had a negative reaction to pro football that was on at the time.

Thomas asked, "Don't they get hurt doing that wrestling?"

"I said, "Yes, but they make a lot of money and their bones ache when they get older."

They said, they like John Wayne, so they chose a DVD called "COWBOYS." They sat intently watching it and Theo as well.

Earlier, I had to tap Theo on the shoulder to say it's been an hour, so he would be aware of the phone time and not talk longer than he expected to. Theo told me that the lady who Sofie used to do housework for told the family that Sofie was "lonely." After hanging up with Sofie, he told me, his sister said that, in fact, she wasn't lonely.

I said, "The lady said that, so you guys would call your sister."

Another day, Thomas came over to ask to use the phone to call a prospective client who may want him to train his horse since Thomas is an Amish horse trainer at twenty years of age.

He paid Ray ten dollars for the past long distance phone calls he made to clients that he corresponded with from Iowa and out of our local area.

He said he went to Lanesboro today to try to sell some calves at an auction, but they wanted too little money for them. He brought them back home. He still lives with his mom, dad, nine brothers and one sister. His older brother, James, had married the Amish woman who was nine years his senior, last year. Remember, James was the one that helped build our addition.

DAY of LEISURE

Out for their Sunday walk, the Amish brothers, Thomas, Theo, and Clay came over again to ask if they could see another John Wayne western movie on TV? It was their day of leisure, but Ray was watching the Packers play football. They marveled at the players, asking how much money do they make?

"Millions, millions!"...said Ray.

I said, "Yeah, they are twenty-five to forty year olds and they really will feel it when they are fifty..."ooh, ugh, ooh!" referring to aches and pains.

After half an hour, they dismissed themselves. I offered them each a soda and they insisted on paying me for it. I refused it because it was a treat from me. Thomas chose a coke. I was surprised because I thought Amish do not drink anything with caffeine. Anyway, Thomas handed a one dollar bill for his two sodas to Ray, anyway. Two of their dogs were patiently waiting for them outside. Our male cat scatted somewhere because he is leery of other people around, much less strange dogs.

THE HORSE SCARE

It was the first of November around 2 PM. Thomas had just come over to use the phone. The neighbor farmers who rent our field were harvesting or pulling field corn. They came through with noisy machinery via our driveway. It scared his horse and buggy that he tied up at the front side fence. I happened to look out the kitchen window as the machinery came by and saw the horse jump and jump up shaking the fence loose. I told Thomas to go check. He ended up tying him to the tree and came back in to use the phone.

He did not mention he was sorry only that "they (the people driving the machinery) don't even stop for anything when they come by."

I called Ray at work so he wouldn't be too alarmed or upset about the fence.

Thomas came back at about 4:45 PM to use the phone again. He brought two different horses and tied them up in a different place out front further from the gate. After his calls, he apologized to Ray and said he would fix the fence after they pull the corn all this week.

I HAD to TELL HER

Just when I thought I was going to have a day to catch up on things like organize a photo album, or take a shower, Sofie came knocking on the door to use the phone. It was good to see her. She was home visiting her parents for two weeks. She needed to use the phone to call someone who she spoke Dutch to. She couldn't get a hold of a couple of people, while I went to work on the computer.

She came in to the room where I was working. I directed her to the window to show her the fence that Thomas's horse broke when the machinery that harvested the field corn came by (explained earlier). I asked her, "Oh, your brother didn't tell you the fence broke....?

She said, "UH, no...?

I found it hard to believe, because she came over walking. Usually she brings her horse and buggy to use the phone. She had no comment, just a sigh, after I explained what happened.

After we walked back into the kitchen, she tried once again to reach her party.

CHAUFFERING THEM into TOWN, and to GENERAL STORE

She then asked, "Do you have time today?"

I responded, "To to do what?"

"I would like to know if you could take me and my mom into town and the General Store?"

"I still needed to shower and do a couple of things around here, I answered. What time would you like to go?"

She said that she would like to go after dinner. Like a good neighbor, I suggested 12:30 PM, and she agreed.

I was there as Sofie, her Mom, and her youngest son, four year old Larry, came out to board the car and go into town. I stressed that they buckle up, because it's the law and you never know if a cop is out there. I parked the car and they went into the bank and so did I, to cash a check.

We went to the thrift shop where Kitty bought a used ironing board. She said that it was to replace the one she had busted. We then headed to the local food center. Once back in the car, Sofie handed me an ice cream sandwich as they were eating one as well. I finished the ice cream, then I drove them through ....., going the back way to the general store owned by the .... I told them, I'd wait for a while and I'll be right in to go looking around. I had been to the general store twice before, once with Kitty when I went in, and once with Sofie when I stayed in the car and waited. Yes, one who drives the Amish must be a patient individual.

I saw that a small Amish woman was going up and down a ladder type extension to an attic getting merchandise and things to restock the shelves. She was the owner, I believe. I asked Ann if she had a snap coin purse? She said, she only had zippered little purses and showed me them. I ended up buying the small, beige leather coin purse to keep my change in for one dollar and eighty cents and two spools of thread, white and off-white for one dollar and eighty cents.

Ann added everything up in her head itemizing what I bought on the carbon copy sales receipt tablet. She used no cash register or calculator. So, it was a slow process. Anyway, she asked me if I would go pick up her daughter, Beatrice, from school? I said that I would.

"How much would you charged me?" she asked softly.

"I said, "Oh, one dollar...oh, fifty cents...oh, that's okay."

She insisted on paying and gave me back two dollars to pay me for picking up her daughter. The little zippered coin purse was paid for.

THE LOCAL SCHOOL HOUSE

I drove over to the schoolhouse across the road from her general store since she showed where it was through the window. I knocked on the schoolhouse door. As I was about to enter, the young Amish teacher in her early twenty's greeted me.

"I am here to pick up Beatrice. Her mom, Ann sent me. Is it time?"

"Yes, it's almost time," she kindly replied.

I waited for six minutes in the coat room. I observed that there were leather baseball mitts hanging on the coat racks as well as the students' coats. I thought that I saw baseballs of sorts, but I can't remember if they were leather or rubber. The eight children (some desks were empty) sitting in their individual desks, sang a closing song as the teacher listened while sitting at her desk. I listened to the words. It was a song of thanking God for this day of learning as school was done and it was time to go home....

I saw two girls getting their coat and asked which one was Beatrice? One acknowledged that she was so we walked out to the car. I asked the four boys and a girl who was going to pick them up. They said that they lived right next door and there they went toward the neighbor house. I told Beatrice to sit in the back seat and buckled her in, as I told her, " We need to be safe."

I brought her to her house next to their general store. I said, "Here you are." I don't remember her saying "Thank you," or I didn't hear it, but she said it with her smile, and walked straight to her house. I went in and told her Mom that she was home. She continued to be waiting for Sofie and Kitty to compile their stuff.

Kitty said, " Sofie is buying toys for the children for Christmas." (referring to her students in WI) I told her I'll be waiting in the car. After about twenty minutes, Sofie started to load the back of the car with boxes of stuff. Sofie and her mom finally came out and walked over to the main house. I waited patiently for another twenty minutes until they came out and got in the car.

"Did you go visiting? I inquired.

"Oh, we went to visit James's wife. She was cooking some meat while James was still at work," replied Kitty.

Relaying this to Ray, he again wonders why they don't invite me in when they go visit someone.

Again, James is Kitty's eldest son who just got married to the general store owners' oldest daughter who was nine years his senior.

It was time to take Kitty and Sofie home as it was almost 4:30 PM.

Kitty, "How much do I owe you?"

I answered, "Oh, four dollars." (for the gas)."

Sofie pulled out four dollars. I realized a while back, I needed to at least ask for that.

HOW MANY GALLONS of ICE CREAM?

Kitty asked me if I could take Sofie into town to buy three gallons of ice cream at the convenience store. I guess, she thought it would be cheaper there than the food center. I said that I could buy it and bring it over. She said to just keep it in the freezer until 5 PM the next day, by dinner, since they didn't have one. Otherwise, it would all melt. The boys could come over and pick up it up. I told her, I better bring it over. What kind of ice cream do you want and how much?

"1 gallon?"… of vanilla?" I asked.

"Oh, 1 gallon wouldn't be enough! We are too many. (twelve kids plus mom & dad.) That wouldn't feed us," answered Kitty.

(We chuckled.)

"Okay, how many gallons of ice cream do you want me to buy?"

"Why don't you buy 1 gallon of vanilla, 1 gallon of strawberry, and 1 gallon of chocolate. By this time Sofie was telling me to get Cookies 'n' Crème. Kitty interjected and said for me to get just chocolate, so they could mix it like "neopolitan" - three flavors. Could I count on you?" she asked firmly.

I assured her, "Of course!" I felt like telling her, I can't count on Thomas though. I don't know if Sofie relayed the fact that he hasn't come over to fix or help fix the fence that his horse yanked out and broke due to the neighbor's heavy machinery coming through as his horse was tied up too close and got spooked.

We unloaded the stuff on the lawn as her sons came out and stood close by to take the goods into the house. Thomas still had that long expression on his face. A penny for his thoughts...(He still needed to make good his word about offering to fix the fence. I assumed they were done "pulling the corn." I still was somewhat disappointed about this.)

The day after Thanksgiving on Friday, Ray & I came from Winona and swung around the convenience store to buy one gallon of vanilla ice cream, one gallon of chocolate ice cream, and half gallon of cookies and cream, since there was no strawberry. Anyway, we ended up going to the food center for the one gallon of strawberry. I kept the receipts and put the containers of ice cream in our workshop freezer until 4:50 PM when I loaded them up into the car to deliver to the Amish. I got out of the car and called to Thomas walking down the path.

"Where is your mom?"

He said his Mom & Sofie went to see a newborn baby of an Amish friend. He called his dad to come out and choose the ones he wanted - vanilla, strawberry, and cookies and cream. He said to keep the chocolate since they may not finish it in time before it melts. (What happened to milkshakes?)

I showed the dad, Alfred, the receipts and added on a calculator to get the total of the prices of the three flavored ice creams. He opens his wallet and gets thirteen dollars and thirteen cents cash to pay me for them. All the while his sons were gathered around him. They gaze at me intently and I know were happy to get the ice cream.

Lo and behold! As I drove away, I saw in the distance an Amish buggy coming from the east toward their house. It had to be Kitty and Sofie making it right on time, just like we agreed at 5 PM. I missed them.

Thomas, Theo, Clay, and Sofie walked over on that Sunday after Thanksgiving to see another cowboy movie. Ray first put on "Quigley Down Under," but they didn't care for it. They asked to see another John

Wayne movie so Ray put "North to Alaska" in the DVD player. They seemed to like that movie better. I offered them popcorn and soda. Our treat!

I always tell them if seeing movies is okay with their parents or if their parents know that they are over here watching movies. Thomas gave me the same answer as before.

"Oh, they think, we are just going for a walk. They don't know," he said.

"Well, I don't want to get you in trouble," as always, is my reply.

On Saturday, when Ray and I returned from Winona, we noticed one of Thomas's horses had jumped the fence, since it was on the county road out of the pasture. As soon as we approached his house before going up the hill and home, Ray parked, waved down, and called out to Thomas.

"You have a horse out of the field."

"Oh, okay, thanks. I'll take care of it," assured Thomas.

I thought what a nice gesture for Ray to do.

DAY of FIXING the FENCE

The next day on Monday, Thomas, Sofie, Jess, and Larry, the little four year old brother came over at around 2:30 PM. Thomas told Ray, he was going to fix the fence. He went to work at it while Sofie walked the boys around to see the sheep and the Emus. I walked out to check on them while everyone was watching their brother work, including the tamed pony which Jess rode over. The cart with a horse was tied up off at the side. Thomas already had the new post of which he continued to saw and nail the boards to recreate that portion of the front fence.

I am hoping Sofie egged him on to finally come over to take care of matters. When he got done, he said he wanted to talked to Ray. We, all, walked over to the house and I called upstairs for Ray who was working "office in the home" that day.

Thomas reassures Ray, "I fixed the fence. It's done. It just doesn't have a middle board."

"Ray says, "OK. Thanks.

I thanked him, too and was so pleased that he came forward to get the job done. It seemed like it was good enough for now. I looked out the kitchen window with Thomas, as Ray went back up the stairs. I told him I wished we could do the whole fence.

Thomas said, "Oh, I like to do that."

"Yeah...? " I said, "but I'd like to redo the whole fence with vinyl fencing."

I offered them all a soda. Thomas lead the horse out of the ditch,

Sofie & little four year old Larry got in the cart, Jess jumped on his pony and off they went down the road to home.

It was the end of November when looking out the kitchen window that I noticed Mickey, the fifteen year son of this Amish family, was tying up his buggy to the giant spruce tree. He came to ask if I would take his mom into town.

I had to stop him and tell him, "Sorry, I have to get ready to go teach an art class to children for community education and can't do it today. The next two Thursdays will be busy, too, since they are my teaching days as well.

I saw the look in his eyes. It was the look of sincerity and sadness that I couldn't help his mom that day.

"Oh, that's Ok, we can get someone else," Mickey politely commented. I asked him if he would like to use the phone to call someone?

"Oh, I don't use the phone." How loyal to the rules of the Amish, he is. Again, I told him I was sorry, I couldn't help. He got back in his horse and buggy and drove down the hill to home to relay the message.

AMISH DO NOT RECYCLE!

Ray and I were wondering where were all the empty cans from the sodas I gave to the kids on the day they watched TV, as well as the day Thomas fixed the fence. Ray's feeling was right. They don't recycle aluminum, since he found some soda cans in the ditch where the fence was rebuilt.

"I guess, they think they are biodegradable and will disappear into the earth," I supposed.

No wonder we see piles of aluminum and metal scrapes in the distant fields of the Amish. One would think they conserve on everything, but don't they know that they can cash in their cans for money?

I remember their mom, Kitty, telling me that one day, when Theo was riding in his buggy, he was stopped by the county sheriff who thought he was littering the road with soda cans. She told me that Theo told her that he was picking up cans, not throwing them around.

"He got a warning from the sheriff, not a citation," I believe, she said.

I listened and did not judge.

I only said, We can't litter the highways and roads. It's against the law."

SOFIE LOST HER JOB

I learned from Thomas, when he came over to use the phone end of the first week of December.

He ask me, "Did you hear what happened to Sofie?"

I am looking at him perplexed. "No, not unless your Mom tells me anything."

"She lost her job. The parents didn't like her for a teacher. The scholars liked her, the kids loved her, but the parents didn't. She just went back, from a two week Thanksgiving vacation with her family here, to get out and gather her stuff."

"Where is she now?

"She is home."

"What happened to all the Christmas gifts she bought her students?"

"She gave some away to the kids and will be able to return some stuff back to the general store."

All I know. she was getting paid forty-five dollars a day in a very small town in north central, Wisconsin. If she got a teaching job here in her local community, she would have been paid only fifteen dollars a day.

Anyway, they still supplied her with a ride home. I told Thomas to tell her to keep her chin up. She can always go back to cleaning house for her lady friend.

CHRISTMAS GIFT for KITTY

The day after Christmas, Thomas came over to use the phone in the early afternoon to call his horse training prospective and current customers. Actually, I thought about delivering a gift a couple days earlier, but wasn't sure if his family would be able to accept gifts.

"Is it ok to get gifts for Christmas? I quizzed Thomas.

"Oh yes, we can, " replied Thomas. I told him to wait five minutes while I put together a Christmas gift for his mom. So, I gathered an apple cinnamon red candle, a couple bars of natural soap, a decorated can of Danish shortbread cookies, and a stuffed bears 2007 calendar. I placed them all in a holiday designed gift bag to go. He thanked me for the gift and as always, thanked me for using the phone.

Ray kept track of the long distance calls when the phone bill came. Thomas will pay for any phone calls that he, Sofie, his mom, or Theo made on our phone. That was made clear.

HERBALS for WEIGHT LOSS

Sofie came over to use the phone, but had to leave a message to call back. She asked if I could "run down and let her know if anyone called back...if you want to." I told her that I would, especially, if it was an emergency.

As it turned out a lady returned the call for "herbal weight loss" products. I, not thinking who Sadie called, (because she never told me) told the lady that I may have dialed the wrong number by mistake trying to call my son. Sometimes, the beep of the number doesn't kick in and a certain number is not entered. She said my name was left on her answer machine. I did write down my phone number and told her to leave our name and number, so someone can call back. Remember, I didn't know at this time who she had called until I figured it out later.

When she came back a few days later to use the phone again, I had asked her if she got her party?

She said, "No."

"Did you leave your name and a number?"

"No..." she sighed.

When I told her a lady selling an herbal weight loss program called back, she confessed she wanted to lose weight. I let her browse in an old catalog for herbal cures, teas, etc. She saw what she was looking for - natural herbal tablets for weight loss. I told her to wait until I got the current magazine in the mail. Ray had suggested early on that I order a new, updated catalog. Apparently, the old catalog showed up in the mail years ago, so I kept it.

Sofie is happy faced by now. Having made progress in her endeavor. Anyway, Sofie hooked up the sled and went back home. (two weeks later, I got my new catalog. Although Sofie didn't let me know yet, I'm sure that she got her catalog in the mail, too. I added her name to the: mail catalog to a friend list.)

NO ACCESS to a COMPUTER

Thomas came over today, Wednesday, January 3, 2007, to call his customers. No one home. Once more, I am trying to be of help.

"Maybe, you can write them. Do you have an address? I remarked.

"It's www......" Thomas answered.

"Oh, that's the world wide website address for the internet," I explained. That is not the mailing address. If you have the "www" address, I can look it up on the computer. It may show the mailing address to write them a letter."

He will ask his mom and dad if they know the website address and let me know next time he comes to use the phone.

SOMETIMES, I HAD TO SAY "NO"

On a Saturday morning in January, Sofie called me to ask, "What are you doing today?"

I told her that I was going into town to get some antibiotics for my cat.

I exclaimed, "Where are you?

She answered, "I am at …..'s place off some road…"

I didn't understand her voice, as she is hard to understand, because of her Dutch/German accent.

"Oh, okay," I continued listening.

I am wondering where she is using the phone from. As a rule, Amish don't have a phone in their home, so they use the phone elsewhere.

Actually, one of my old mama cats needed some antibiotics, since she was having a hard time breathing. She possibly had pneumonia or it's her heart according to what the vet assistant said when I called early that morning. My cat was just laying around for days, but still was drinking water and eating. More than six months ago, she had a kidney or bladder infection and antibiotics cured her to the point she started eating again.

Anyway, Sofie wanted to see if I'd "take her mom into ….. to get a piece of furniture at the Salvation Army."

When I told her I had to go into ….., she said, "Wait a minute, I have a friend here. Let me ask her if she wants to go to ….. As I waited a moment, she returned to say, "No, we'll just let it go."

I told her, "Sorry, I can't take her mom into ....., since I have to care for my cat and go get medicine for her."

"THANKS for THE PHONE"

Thomas, the twenty year old Amish horse trainer, came over one day to use the phone.

Before he entered the front yard, I quickly asked Ray, "What does he owe for his phone bill?"

Ray looked at the telephone statement, tallied it up and said that it was less than twenty dollars.

Thomas approached the back porch door to the kitchen, knocked and asked to use the phone.

After he was done, Ray said, "Oh, the telephone bill is about twenty."

Thomas said, "Oh, the bill will get paid. Well, thank you for me using the phone."

All we could say was, "OK."

Once again, on a snowy day in February, we saw him coming up the driveway and as usual tied his horse to the front, outer fencing in the ditch.

Ray noticed, "Amish are here! I think it's Thomas."

"Ray, what does Thomas owe for the phone?" I exclaimed. Ray gathered the phone statement again and figured it was exactly seventeen dollars and twenty-nine cents.

I opened the back porch-kitchen door and greeted him. I noticed he had already popped off his outer rubber boots. I offered Thomas to come in and sit down at the kitchen table.

"Oh, that's OK, I can call in here (back porch)," he said. He proceeded to make his calls like he always did in the back porch.

"Hi, ...this is Thomas, the horse trainer..."

I couldn't help but overhear his telephone greeting to whomever he was calling.

When he got done, he opened the door and told me that he was done making phone calls.

He said, "My Mom went to a funeral in northern Iowa because her cousin's husband died. He went into the chicken house, came back in the house and just died. I think he had a "clot.""

"Oh, I'm sorry. She went in this weather? I inquired. It's blowing out there!" (I was picturing her in the horse and buggy.)

"Oh, she went anyway," he added.

It dawned on me, "Ah, someone drove her there." Thomas confirmed that she was driven by a driver. (Good thing, she had her adult daughter Sofie who minded the eight minor children while she was gone.)

Before he was getting ready to leave, I kindly told him, "Oh, your phone bill is seventeen dollars and twenty-nine cents."

"Oh, OK, I'll tell my sister, he proclaimed. Thanks for letting me use the phone. Bye."

Saying bye to him, I thought to myself (why does he need to tell his sister? I mentioned that thought to Ray.

"Maybe, he thinks she is going to pay the bill..." Ray mumbled.

She did make a few calls herself.

COW on the RUN

It was Saturday midday. Ray looked out the window and shouted, "There's a cow on the loose!" Lo and behold, I saw what turned out to be a young black calf running from south to north on our road. Chasing the calf was fifteen year old Jess. Good thing, he was pacing himself by running and walking to keep up with the little cow.

"Ray, go be a hero," I suggested humorously.

Jess needs help catching that cow. How was he going to catch it. He had no rope. Ray went out to block it from going any further down the road. The calf saw Ray standing there and made a right angle turn into our driveway. It kept being elusive until it got caught up in the north pasture. Jess shut the gate while Ray went to get some rope in the workshop.

I looked away from the northeast washroom window for a minute and I saw the calf running into the driveway from the road again! It must have jumped the barbed wire pasture, into the ditch and on to the driveway (confirmed by Ray, later).

All of a sudden, I heard more voices yelling in all this commotion. It turned to be Thomas on his horse and Jess's younger brother, Rudy, and their little dog barking. The calf must have gone around the house twice. Again, my eyes left for a minute. Then, from the kitchen, I saw Thomas on his horse through the north washroom window. He had stopped and I was wondering exactly what was going on. I went to look out the northeast washroom window and Ray has tackled the calf. Then,

I looked moments later and Thomas has wrestled the calf, applying his body strength by bearing down.

Somehow, in all this, they managed to grab the calf by his tail and back, lead him down the driveway and finally down the road toward their farm. Thomas remounted his horse and got the calf to run forward. Jess and Rudy hurried into the south pasture, to be ready, in case the calf strayed again. They, then, disappeared in the distance. What an escapade!

"PAID" a VISIT

It was the last day of February and Sofie startled me with a tap on the kitchen door. She came with her fourteen year old, little brother Jess.

When she asked to use the phone, she remarked, "How much do I owe you...seventeen dollars?"

"Actually, it is twenty-one dollars, because the new bill came," I said.

"Oh, okay," agreed Sofie, as she handed me a twenty dollar bill. I'll owe you one dollar."

I went back to the computer. I decided to go and ask Jess, if I could take some pictures of the Shetland ponies harnessed to the flat bed that they came in. They had a bale of hay to sit on the flat bed, as I later asked them what it was for.

I helped Sofie find a phone number by calling information. The last name wasn't listed in the phone directory. Apparently, when I called the operator for information, she said the name, but we got the "ie" switched around. Anyway, the name was still not listed in the phone book. It was still a success.

Sofie got her party. She told me, she was going to sell her baked goods at the Farmers Market in Winona on the weekend. What a deal! She sounded happy and elated about the opportunity.

She and Jess loaded up on the flatbed pulled by the two Shetland ponies. Off they went, down the driveway, back home down the hill.

"NOW, I am a HANDFUL!"

Sofie came knocking on a Tuesday, one day before the first day of spring. Ninety per cent of the snow has melted off with twenty degrees Fahrenheit at night and thirty-five degrees Fahrenheit during the day. Anyway, I saw, she brought her little brother, Larry, the youngest of the children.

I wondered and questioned, "Where is the wagon and the horses. I don't see them anywhere."

"Oh, Thomas dropped me off," explained Sofie.

"Oh, is he running the horses?" I concluded.

"Yeah, he is going to come back," she said.

She came to use the phone, but asked me while I was on the computer, if I knew the "Chatfield" phone number. No one was picking up. She wanted to make sure she was dialing the right number and if it was a cell phone number? I looked up a Chatfield listing on our computer copy of the monthly phone bill where we highlight all the Amish calls in yellow. She recognized it and was dialing the right number. I was not sure if the party she was trying to reach used a cell phone. She finally, after a third try, got a hold of someone, but the person she wanted to talk to wasn't home until the afternoon.

"She is getting her hair done," Sofie told me.

I asked Larry, "So, how are you doing?"

A few seconds passed.

Good...are you good?" I continued.

He stared at my face in wonder.

Sofie, done with the phone, walked over and supportively said kindly, "He doesn't understand you."

"How old are you?" I showed him four fingers. He put up five fingers, showing me that he was five years old, as he subtly smiled. He, finally, knew that he understood something I said or asked.

"Do you go to school yet?" I continued trying to converse with little Larry.

Sofie and I moved over to gaze out the kitchen window.

"But I thought he understands English. Don't you speak to him in English?" I inquisitively asked Sofie.

"No," said Sofie, "He doesn't learn English until he is seven years old and goes to school." We speak to him in Dutch.

Sofie told me, "Larry was sitting around the other day at home in a chair, just thinking. He mentioned, 'I am five years old - today! Now, I am a handful!'"

We both couldn't help not to chuckle.

"A handful! Not quite," I commented assuredly.

I gave him an orange. He again looks, but does not say anything. He was hesitant, but I insisted he could have it. I don't know if he didn't want it, or was looking for a big enough pocket to put it in. I think, it was the latter.

Looking at Larry, I said, "Oh, let me give Sofie an orange, too!" She thought, she heard Thomas drive by, so she went to check. She came back in and said it wasn't him.

A few minutes later he arrived with the flatbed wagon. (Thomas trains horses and runs them now and again.) As Sofie and little brother Larry stepped down into the back porch, I told her that she is going to have to teach me how to speak Dutch.

"How do you say 'Bye' in Dutch?" I asked.

"The same, 'Bye,'" she clarified.

"Hello?"

"Hi. It's the same as English."

I waved to Sadie in a split second from the kitchen window and waved again. She motioned to Thomas and he turned his head to the window. I waved with a smile and he waved back. Off, they went.

TRAINING and SELLING HORSES

Thomas came over early on the 5th of April to call someone to buddy with to take his horses to the auction sale in Lanesboro, MN.

"The guy wasn't home," Thomas said.

"So, how much do you sell your horses for?" I asked.

"Oh, for $800 to $1000 each, riding or work horse. Another little colt was born yesterday," he happily exclaimed.

That makes it two little ponies were born from mid March to beginning April. He just loves his horses, hence he is a horse trainer. From time to time, I see Thomas running the horses up and down the road in a buggy or some sort of hitched on carriage or flatbed.

The first year we met Thomas, he asked Ray if he could help him haul his horses down the road to get castrated by another Amish man who specialized in the procedure. So Ray hooked his sheep trailer to his truck and went to lend a hand. This was a "prepaid" or bartered favor, since he returned it by taking care of the sheep, emus, and cats while we went to California and Nevada for a week.

Anyway, that was the day when Ray came back at lunch time. I thought he was done, but he still had to go back, load the horses and take them all back to Thomas's pasture, bleeding and all. I know, it sounds gross. I learned that's how the horses were sterilized. Ray mentioned that his brakes went out, but was able to drive the truck and trailer back safely.

PUSHED DOWN by a HORSE

Thomas came to use the phone once again to call some of his clients or owners of the horses that he trained. He couldn't get a hold of anyone and proceeded to let me know that he was done using the phone. He stepped into the leaving room. He smelt of a foul, germy odor.

"I am sick. I have a cold. I can't get a hold of anyone," said Thomas.

"You can try later," I assured him.

"I don't think so, not today. I don't feel good. My stomach is all messed up. I have been coughing out pus. One of my horses that I was trying to trim his hair (mane), jumped up and pushed me back real hard on my chest with his front legs," he said sadly.

"If you have a cold, you need to drink a lot of water, tea with honey, or orange juice to keep full of fluids. Maybe, eat some of your Mom's applesauce and crackers, if your stomach is upset. You should see the doctor. You might need antibiotics. You should rest yourself, because even when you start feeling good, you may have a relapse or go back to feeling sick," I explained.

"Oh, I can't, because I have to wait for someone to help me shoe the horses today. . .Ok...anyway, thanks for letting me use the phone," he said while making his exit to the back porch door.

The next day on a Sunday at almost 10:00, he came with his brother Clay and their little Jack Russell terrier dog to use the phone. I had this premonition that they wanted to watch a movie. Yes, I was right!

After Thomas was done with phone, he asked, "Can we watch a movie?"

I firmly said, "Well, I have to do some things first. Why don't you come back at around 12:30 or 1:00 in the afternoon?"

"OK, we'll come back then," they answered in unison.

FRESH BAKED GOODS

Sofie asked me on the third Monday of April, if I could take her to sell her baked goods at the park in ….., "if I had time?" She was going to go home and start baking bread, rolls, cookies, and bars so she could set up a table and sell her goods.

I told her, "OK. What time?"

"Oh, whatever time you'd like?" she responded.

"What time do you need to be there?" I asked again.

"How about nine o' clock your time? The eight o' clock, my time."

I said, "OK." So, it was settled.

She had asked me if I could make some signs to pin up at the local food center and convenience store in town. I gave her a piece of paper to write what she wanted on the sign.

"Is it OK to write "FRESH" baked goods on the sign?" I inquired.

"Yes, of course," she confirmed.

She left back home in her horse drawn carriage that she had tied to our huge maple tree. I went to work, typing out and printing five poster-flyers to advertise the sale for passersby to notice and, maybe, run over to the park and buy her baked products.

I got there about 8:50 on Wednesday morning to pick her up. Sofie directed me to park the car closer to the side door, so she and her brother could load the bakery goods closer and easier in my SUV. She invited me in. I told her I made her signs. She wanted me to bring them in, so she could see one.

"The sign needs to have "Farmers Market" on it, so no one can say anything. I will be safe," she said.

Do you have a big felt pen, so I can write that on the signs?" I asked.

I went back to the car to get the five - 8 ½ X 11 inch posters and a bigger sign that I made out of a cardboard box. She gave me a huge, black marker and I edited all the signs.

When I found out Theo was going to keep Sofie company, I said, "Oh, I wasn't sure if you were going alone or taking somebody with you... I don't think we have room for another person, if I have to pull down by back seats to fit everything."

"You didn't think I was going to be alone, did you?" she commented.

"We will see, " I consoled.

We went back to my car and juggled our space around. We were good to go as soon as Theo and Sofie loaded up the fresh baked goods.

We drove from their driveway up the road toward the highway. I asked about the newly built "chicken farm building" across from them. I was not sure who was tending to it. Sofie said that their neighbor, Richard, built it for his children to tend to the raising and feeding of the chickens. It is an egg farm as well. What a sense of responsibility for the children.

"If there's a will, there's a way," Sofie mentioned.

"That's one of my sayings," I said. My mom would always say that."

We delivered the posters accordingly in town, but had to go to the next town where they could set up their bake sale in the park. Sofie said on the way that she didn't bring any lunch, but some rolls to eat. Anyway, we stopped to see if any shops were open to post a sign for a day. It was already 10:00 and no one was open, yet. How weird. We arrived at the park to unload the baked items. I told her I would pin up a poster at the convenience store in ….. as well.

"Could you buy some orange soda for us to drink? I forgot to bring something to drink! I'll pay you for it."

I said that I would.

She also needed to go to the restroom. She mentioned at this time that she called the town's city hall earlier to see if it would be all right to set up her baked goods stand. The city hall said it would be OK any time she wanted to. After driving around the small residential type town looking for the city hall for her to use the restroom, I remembered where the veterinarian's office was located. I told her that she could go in there to ask to use the restroom and also, ask where city hall was? Sure enough, she did. I drove her around the block and left her with Theo to sell her goods at the park.

I was to pick them up at four o' clock, my time. I was there at 4:15 PM. Sofie had some customers buy, but didn't sell enough, yet. She asked if I could wait around for a while so she could sell more baked goods when the car traffic came by. I told her that I couldn't, because I had to go home and cook.

So we packed up and drove home. In our conversation, she told me she walked to the craft shop across the street from the park where she set up her stand. The owner opened up, but explained to her that his wife was in the hospital or had surgery, so he didn't open up as his sign said, "open."

I got to thinking she could try to sell her baked goods at the assisted living home, the convenience store, the food center, or the café closer to home. I told her that when I went back home after I left them off, I noticed no Amish or anyone selling anything in our local city park in town. Why couldn't she sell there? It would be closer and she would get more buyers. She told me some other Amish group has reserved through city hall, but they won't be able to start until May.

Anyway, Sofie and Theo went in the assisted living center and asked if they would be interested in any baked goods.

Sofie came out and said, "They might buy, but we have to wait a few minutes to see what the manager says."

She asked me if I wanted bread or a pie for my helping her. I told her that apple pie would be great. She placed one in the front seat. Meanwhile, the manager of assisted living drove up shortly, greeted them, and walked them into the building... No luck.

Sofie explained, "The manager said they can't buy any, because of a state rule (regulation).

I guess, their baked goods are not approved for consumption, in my opinion. I consoled Sofie by telling her, it's not that they don't trust you or what you put in the baked goods. It's just the state's rule. The manager of the assisted living center suggested they try the resource center in town.

I remarked, "You won't just give them away. They need to pay you for them, right?"

She definitely agreed. I told her we might as well not go to the convenience store or the food center, because they will want your label with ingredients, dates and package weight, etc. for the fresh baked goods. I stopped by the café. Sofie and Theo went in, but came back to the car. It was a "No" there as well. I, then, drove them to the resource center. They entered. The outcome was again, to no avail.

Sofie said, "They asked if we wanted to donate the food?"

"They get money from the county. You'd think they could pay for fresh baked goods. Then, they end up giving it away," I muttered.

I drove them home. Sofie paid me for the gas as I told her up front that I would charge her six dollars to take her and bring her home. (I had planned to charged her one dollar and fifty-nine cents for the orange soda, and four dollars for making the signs for a total of eleven dollars and fifty-nine cents. Oh, well.) She asked if I wanted a loaf of white bread or..?

"Oh, do you have wheat bread?" I replied.

"Yes, here," handing me the loaf.

"Thank you. Now, I know who makes pies and if I need pies…" I said.

Sofie adds, "Could you keep the pies in your freezer until Saturday? I want to try to sell on Saturday."

"I guess, but you have to remind me on Friday evening or come pick them up."

I, ultimately, brought them home in trays along with four batches of cinnamon rolls which were selling at two dollars each. She went from seven to six dollars each for the pies. Since the Amish have no electrical outlets to keep a refrigerator or freezer in order to store their meat or bakery goods, I thought, I'd help them out a little. I did see that they have portable, hand coolers.

All in a day's work! She said she was baking from 3:00 - 9:00 PM the night before.

Sofie came over in a buggy on Thursday about 7:00 PM to call someone to take her to the park to sell her baked goods on Saturday. Theo waited in the buggy for a while until I noticed that he was talking on the phone to someone. I went back to the computer and Sofie came to tell me they got someone.

I walked her over to the kitchen and Theo stayed in my bedroom/computer room watching TV. I know he was marveled by watching TV. I told her that Ray went to Wisconsin to work on his rental some more as the new tenants will be moving in soon and new carpet will be installed this weekend.

I told her, "I am used to being alone. My dad died when I was fifteen years old and my mom, also, got used to being alone. She is tough.

We gazed out at the southern pastures to see the farm in the distance. Sofie said that she went to rake leaves for the house behind that farm. That is where they hold Sunday church. We moved into the room where Theo was still watching TV. Of course, he was standing, not sitting, the whole time. Sofie started watching TV while I began reading my e-mail. After the program was done, I shut the computer off and walked into the kitchen. That was cue enough for them to know it was time to leave.

Sofie rushed out, "Well, bye now." See you later."

They rode out. They were going to pick up the pies about 9:00 on Saturday morning.

SUGGESTIONS for the
AMISH COUNCIL

IF I could present myself as a civilian outsider to the Amish Community Council, whenever they have their meetings, I would with good intentions and innovative ideas. One of my proposals would be for each Amish household to have use of, at least, one cell phone for business purposes. They are battery operated, not run by electricity.

Sofie's Amish Community should have access or be allowed to buy a parcel or half acre of land near a highway. This would allow the Amish to establish their true, homemade food and craft stands to be available to their community and all public alike. I say "true" because a local business just uses the name "Amish" in the naming of their restaurant-gift shop when it is not, in fact, run by the Amish.

Three and two years ago, I sold some of my fresh garden, big beef tomatoes and butternut squash to our local food center. I had also sold some to another small town ten miles south of here and tried to sell some more three weeks later to that same store. The produce manager told me that an Amish girl just sold her four flats of big tomatoes. I respect the business ventures of the Amish. By the same token, I ended up giving my tomato produce away to friends around and in town businesses like the doctor's and dental office where I frequent.

I really wonder why local business will not buy fresh baked goods from the Amish. OK, there is the state regulation, seemingly not trusting the ingredients they use in their baking or cooking. However, the Amish use no preservatives. I guess, businesses fear that people will complain or sue for allergic reactions and what not. Who knows?

Another idea is for the Amish to learn about recycle aluminum especially soda cans. Ray found two root beer soda cans thrown in the back near the pasture.

He knew that Thomas and Clay must have thrown them there.

"Don't they know that aluminum will not disintegrate? It will take years for it to break up into the ground," asserts Ray.

Thomas, Jess, along with Sofie have left empty aluminum cans in the ditch before, when Thomas fixed the fence. That was the time his horse yanked and broke the fence when heavy machinery came through, since we rent the land to harvest field corn.

We need to tell the Amish community that recycling aluminum cans can be, not only a helpful asset to the environment, but a money making hobby for their children.

VISITING WITHOUT NOTICE

The day after Memorial Day, I was in the shower, and Ray came tapping on the bathroom door.

"Sofie and Theo are here, do you want your clothes near?"

I was astounded. He laid my teal romper on the toilet seat, so I would be able to reach it. I guess, he could have told them to come back later. Anyway, Sofie and Theo were here as I stepped out and went upstairs to get a denim shirt to put over my strapless romper. I came down to the kitchen, where Sofie was sitting and Theo was standing.

"Hello," I greeted them.

Looking at Theo's face, I didn't notice until a few minutes later that he had his right hand and arm in a bandaged sling with pins in his fingers. He explained that he cut the tip, including bone, of his right thumb with a chainsaw at work while building an outhouse. He was in surgery for a five hour operation and had some pins put in his right middle fingers to make sure they healed okay. He had to change his bandage every night.

"It's awful, but things happen sometimes so we can become more careful when we are working or doing things," I consoled.

Sofie was sitting at the kitchen table, looking sad because she didn't get her party on the telephone. Still, she never asked me for a ride anywhere…

Sofie got up, rushed out the kitchen door to the back porch door, and said, "Bye."

This was the day Ray planted two cherry trees. I mentioned it to her as I saw her and Theo out the door.

"I was telling Ray that I already smell cherries when I am close by the trees. Maybe, it's psychological," I told her.

Sofie replied, "But, it's going to take a long time."

I thought…no wonder the Amish do not grow trees, a conclusion I came to since one does not see any huge trees by their old or new houses. I wonder if they cut trees down for lumber or burning logs before they build or buy a house? Nature will water them, so they wouldn't need to do that.

Around a little past 6:00 PM on a Wednesday, I recognized the car of the driver that also takes Sofie to the park where she sets up her "Farmers Market" bakery goods stand. I told Ray about this. He went immediately to find out.

Coming in, Ray said, "Sofie wants to know, if there is room in the freezer until Saturday?"

I, promptly, ask Ray if we had any room left in the freezer?

At the same time, I saw her in the back porch.

"I have seven pies and five or six loaves of bread," Sofie confirmed.

Ray took her to the freezer in the workshop, since I told him that she didn't know exactly where it was. Theo knew, because he unloaded them before. Anyway, Sofie went to the car and brought in seven glazed donuts for us. I pointed to my hips.

"We can't eat them all at our house," she proclaimed.

… and I suppose she thinks, we can. Ray mentioned later that he would have rather received a loaf of bread instead! I told him that he needed to tell her that right away if he wants bread.

To really call it "visiting without notice" is when she came over to use the phone. I was on the computer. I had the back porch/kitchen door open. All of a sudden, I heard something or someone in the house. I went to the kitchen and saw Sofie holding the phone.

"I didn't see anyone, so I went to get the phone," she confidently said.

"Oh...," I calmly responded. I go back to the computer.

A few minutes later, she stepped into the living room and I turned my head toward her.

"Well, thanks for using the phone," Sofie said with a soft smile.

I guess, Ray and I will expect to be visited without notice from the Amish.

OLD HORSE GOING HOME

I was in the garden when I heard, then noticed an old, black horse trotting south down the road with his harness dragging. I called loudly to Ray to come and look! It sure seemed like he was trying to find his way back home. Ray got in his car and drove to see. He came back and said that someone in a car with an Amish guy acknowledged the loose horse. Ray, at least, attempted to save the horse. Before I knew it, an Amish boy on a horse was bringing the runaway horse back.

I hollered to him, "He just wanted to go home."

The boy replied, "That's right. That's right."

Ray and I deducted that the Amish were blackberry picking in a pasture down the road like they do this time every year.

JUST DON'T GET the HINT

We were getting ready to sit down and eat dinner, when Thomas dropped Sofie off to use she phone. She told us she had plenty of bakery goods left from her Saturday sale at the park fifteen miles away. She was perhaps, hinting to us, if we wanted to buy some. We weren't interested in any. She didn't even ask if we would store them in the freezer. I suggested that she could sell them at the Amish General Store. She said that they wouldn't buy them. (Ray and I, later thought, there is always the Sunday church gathering. She shouldn't bake too much, but just enough to sell at the park each time.)

Waiting for a call back from one of her customers. Sofie said, "A car with two kids and a girl came down their driveway. They looked drunk. They were driving crooked down the path and swaying side to side. Thomas yelled at them and asked what they were doing? They said, 'We're just looking for goats.' "

Ray mentioned to Sofie that maybe they are looking for stuff like copper to steal. That has been occurring around the rural areas lately. Standing in the living room doorway, Sofie murmured, "I am waiting for Thomas to pick me up. He is running (training) a horse."

The phone rang. Sofie got it and handed it to me. All this time, we were sitting down getting ready to have dinner. The phone was for her, so I handed it back to her. She stepped out to get her call. Her breath reeked of an odor between bad breath and cold germs! Breathing through my mouth, I had that yucky taste in my mouth and smell in my nose for one hour after she left. I do not think, she practices good oral hygiene, since she does wear dentures. I am positive the smell was cold germs though. I would hope, she makes sure her hands are clean when she rolls her dough. Just a thought.

Before Thomas, finally, drove up with horse and trailer, she thought it proper to ask if she could pick our blackberries out in the north woods past the meadow. We let her pick the plums the last two years. She did not hesitate to ask.

Ray said, "Yes, just save some for us," smiling.

"I guess, it would take a lot of blackberries to make a pie," he commented to me later.

All this time, Ray and I wondered why the Amish came around to use the phone from 5:30 - 6:30 PM when we were getting ready to eat dinner? I thought, we should tell them exactly what times they could use the phone, because they didn't seem to excuse themselves when they knew we were getting ready to sit down and eat.

It was Saturday evening around 6 PM when Sofie came by and I was watering the garden. She had someone drive her over.

"I'm over here," exclaiming, so she'd noticed where I was.

"Can I put some of my baked goods in the freezer?" she inquired confidently.

"You will have to ask Ray…he's in the house," I answered.

Sofie knocked and asked Ray. He took her and Clay with the pies, cookies and bread, etc. to unload them in our freezer in the workshop. I observed that an Amish older woman got out of the back seat to get in the front passenger seat. They, then, drove off to go home. I noticed the driver was an elderly woman.

Ray said, she planned to pick up her baked goods, not this, but next Friday. Now, think…Hot goods being all day at the park and in the car in July! Wouldn't they spoil when you put hot food right away in the freezer?

It was Monday. Clickety, click, click, click clack! It was 6:45 AM and the Amish were coming...so, I was thinking as I was waking up. Ray already went to work in the city. I looked out the bedroom window and I saw one of Sofie's brothers looking where to tie up his horse and small cart. I went back to bed. Next thing, I knew, I heard a knock at the door. (I am not answering the door. It's too early! Besides, I'd have to throw something on real fast.) Whoever it was, left after five persisting knocks. I saw him drive off.

At about 5:30 PM, Thomas rode over on his horse to use the phone. I found out through him, that it was Clay who came to use the phone in the morning after I explained, I heard a knock and saw one of his brothers drive off.

Anyway, on this same day, in just two days after Sofie unloaded her baked goods, she came over to knock at the door about 7:00 PM and asked Ray, if she could take some baked goods out of our freezer? I was under the impression, she was taking all of them out. Ray said that she wanted only three pies. They were probably bought by the lady that drove her over.

On Tuesday, about 7:00 PM, Theo rode over with a miniature horse and cart to use the phone to call a friend. After he hung up the phone, he said that he had to call back.

"The weather sure is nice," he began.

"It is suppose to rain on Thursday," I affirmed.

Theo had time to ask us if we were going to be home on Thursday, so he could come over to watch TV. Ray and I looked at each other.

Ray said, "I am not going to be here. I don't think that would be a good idea."

I said, "I do not know what my schedule will be ...We can't do that."

Theo adds, "That's OK."

He showed us his right hand with no pins in three fingers. He got the last one out today. He said that one fell out some time ago. It appeared to be healing pretty nicely. The top of his first thumb joint was gone, but we could see where the rest of the thumb was sown back on at the hospital. He said that there was a blood vessel, so it was saved.

He went to call his friend and talk with him outside for about fifteen minutes. After he was done, he told me that he had been shellacking chairs. I told him about a circular table top I needed legs for. He said that maybe two by fours could be used for legs. I told him not to think too hard on it. He drove home.

Ray said, " We can't let them think we have a movie theater here whenever they want."

NEVER on a RAINY DAY

Sofie came over with Jess to use the phone. It was Wednesday, the first of August and Sofie couldn't get a hold of anyone to drop her off and pick her up that Saturday, so she could sell her fresh baked goods. She had just got back from visiting her grandfather in Iowa for ten days. So, guess what?

"Are you busy Saturday?" she asked.

I am thinking…it would be the second time that I drove her so she could sell. It seems, she didn't know it was going to rain, when she did her baking on Friday.

"Okay, I guess, I can drive you over to the park on Saturday. What time do you need me there?" I asked.

"Oh, I need you to be there at about 8:00 in the morning and to pick me up at 5:00 in the afternoon," she continued.

Saturday morning came. It was starting to rain as was predicted on the weather forecast, but remember the Amish have no TV. I wondered if the Amish folk listen to a battery operated radio to get the weather report or is that a priority in their daily work schedule. Like the saying goes, "Work rain or shine."

Anyway, at a quarter 'til eight, I ate a bowl of cereal and arrived to pick her up at 8:05, slightly late. In about five minutes Danny, her buff, little seven year old brother, brought out the prop up signs and set them by the car and went back in the house. Five minutes later, Sofie steps out barefoot.

"Oh, it will be just a bit," she hollered, as I sat in the car waiting.

Now, I am thinking is it going to be a half an hour wait? I am looking at the scenery around the farm. I see brown young cows in a pen. The father, Alfred, is sweeping off some heavy gray metal machinery. I wasn't sure what it was. His two older boys are standing near the entrance to the dairy barn.

She finally came out with her trays of baked bread, rolls, cookies, and pies. She started loading the back of the car.

"I think you have enough room for your brother," I projected.

She told me that we needed to pick up a lady friend who was going to help her sell. By the time we loaded all the baked goods, stuffed my SUV tightly from side to side, we did not know where to put the table.

Alfred said, "We can tie it down on top of the car with twine."

"I do not have any twine," I said.

"I do," he affirmed. He went to the barn to get some.

Alfred and Sofie loaded the long table upside down on top of the car and tied it down with rope twine, we were ready to go.

"We do not want to scratch the car," Alfred kindly commented.

"Sofie, watch your dad tie the knots, so you know how to undo them. I do not know knots, especially the fancy ones," I admitted.

"I don't do knots," Alfred mentioned. He looped, tied, and pulled securely around the rack on top of my car. Sofie observed her dad.

She hopped in the car with her bowl filled with cereal and milk, a cinnamon roll and a plastic spoon to go, and buckled up. I drove around the circle drive. She is started to eat her cereal.

"How many dairy cows, do you have?" I inquired.

"We have eight dairy milk cows. Just enough milk for our big family," Sofie answered.

I asserted, "Before we go pick up your friend, I am going to let Ray see if we are okay with the table tied on top of the car just to be sure. Which way does your friend live?"

She told me the direction, so I would know which way to go after we went to check with Ray. At this point she said that she needed to go back and get her shoes! I thought, she already put her shoes on when she boarded my car. Her long dress disguises that element.

We drove up to the house. Ray was outside and said we were good to go. We went back to get her shoes and on to pick up her friend. Sofie wanted me to stop at this poultry processing building so she could get down and buy some fifty cent can sodas as she thought it was cheaper there. We arrived at her friend's house. A smaller, shorter Amish woman around thirty-eight to forty-two years old boarded the backseat of the car, toting her lunch in a small cooler and some light blankets to sell.

"I thought something was wrong, since it was getting late," Emily remarked, as she got in the car. We can sell crafts, too, right?" speaking to Sofie.

"Oh, yes," replied Sofie.

Emily directed me how to get to the highway from her place. I knew my way to the park once I got there. On the way, we saw two other Amish women in the first town, who set up their own Farmers' Market in an empty lot.

"Honk your horn," Sofie exclaimed, as she wanted them to see her pass by."

I honked my horn, but told her, "I normally don't like to honk, because other drivers think they are doing something wrong."

We arrived at the town with the park where Sofie was, again, going to have her baked goods sale. I stopped, so she could prop her sign near the highway and then I parked close to the covered tables, so we could unload her items. It was still raining heavily.

"Maybe, we can keep the table on top of your car, since there are tables here," she pondered.

I affirmed, "I think you should take your table down, just in case the authorities need you to use your table. They may say the tables at the park are for public parties." Emily agreed.

She unraveled the twine from the top of my car and we carefully lifted the table onto the ground.

I wished them luck on their sales and said that I would pick them up at 5:00 PM like she wanted. I mentioned that Ray & I were going to be gone shopping from 10:00 AM to 3:00 PM. I drove off back home.

I convinced Ray to help me get through this day after I explained that the car had been overloaded with the table on top. I needed him to take the van and to load the table. Plus, we would all fit better coming back.

It was 4:15 PM and Ray said, "It's still raining hard. Let's go pick Sofie and her friend up now. They are not going to want to stay out there any longer."

I agreed.

Ray cleared out the van and off we went. We arrived at the park. Sure enough, they were happy to see us.

"Ready to pack it up?" I exclaimed. I saw that there were unsold baked items left.

Ray mentioned to them, "I woke up this morning and I knew it was going to rain all day."

He was trying to give them food for thought or a hint as to why they decided to sell that day.

Sofie added, "Since I brought my friend, I had time to sit and listen to her. She gave me the what for…"

Did you have any customers? I asked.

Emily said, "We had four customers all day and we were getting

76

cold. We are glad you came. The rain didn't let up. I have sold stuff before, but we didn't have rain like this. It was sunny then."

We packed up and had to drop off Emily first since that was the sensible route to take. She directed Ray to her home, reversing the route she gave me going away from her home to the highway.

Emily said, "Sofie says she will pay for the trip."

I said, "Oh, Okay… Nice meeting you."

She seemed like a nice, reasonable lady. She was an older, wiser woman that Sofie.

Sofie wanted us to wait, since she went in with Emily and out came another woman of the house with her daughter who bought some of the baked goods.

After Sofie boarded, "Do you think you could stop by a couple places on the way home?"

Ray responded, "How far is it?"

"One place is on the way and the other is a little farther," she concluded.

"I'd rather not. I'd like to get home," Ray continued.

We arrived at a house "on the way" in the Amish neighborhood where Sofie first wanted us to stop. She went to inquire if the lady of the house wanted to but any baked goods. The woman came out with some of her children and bought several loaves of bread, cinnamon rolls, etc.

Sofie came up to me sitting in the van and said something like…

"At least, they bought a lot…not like 'your people…'"

She then got back in the van. I wasn't ready to analyze the statement that she made.

"How much money do I owe you? Sofie asked Ray.

Ray looked at me. I showed him six fingers even though it should have been eight to ten dollars, because of the gas price hike. The van used more gas per mile.

"Oh, six dollars," he told her. She paid for the monthly phone usage of long distance and her portion of the local service charge of the bill, as well. It totaled out to $19.55. She gave me a twenty dollar bill and I gave her back a dollar bill, since I didn't have change. Oh well.

We were nearing her house a quarter mile away, yet.

"Why don't you sell your fresh, baked goods to your Amish neighbors from your buggy?" I inquired.

"That won't work, because they won't buy since they baked themselves," Sofie quickly answered.

We dropped her off and Ray helped her unload the trays of baked goods and her table. She asked if we wanted anything like bread. I told her that Ray would probably like some wheat bread, so she gave him a loaf of bread and cookies.

When Ray and I got home we discussed several things. It was not a good weather day to sell at the park in the first place. Sofie baked too much goods. The Amish won't buy her items. We, personally, thought the cookies were too doughy or more breaded. I guess, one can't be too choosy when some things are given to one. Ray thinks she will not do it this way again, or hopefully, not ask us again. If she does, she shouldn't bring a friend. That person should pay for her ride as well.

The moral to this story is not to over baked more goods than you can sell and don't go, if you think, it's going to rain all day. She had to know, we would not be able to store any extra goods because we have our freezer already full.

JUST FESS UP

I don't know what's worst. Lying, appearing oblivious, or just trying to be clever by not saying anything happened. The second to the last time Thomas came to use our phone, he rode over on his saddled horse and tied it to the four foot post outside the front property in the ditch. This is where we told him to tie his horse, since it yanked a piece of the main fence long before.

Okay, well, Ray noticed in the last week of August, 2007, that the post was slanting over so he redug and reset the post yesterday September 2nd. Why didn't Thomas say anything or just fess when he came to use the phone? I met him at the porch door.

"As I handed him the phone, "Do you want to use the phone?

"Yep," he answered." He brought a two horse, flat bed buggy.

I gathered, he was done making all his contact horse training calls to his clients after half an hour when I saw the phone hung up on the kitchen wall. I was busy in the house, since I didn't hear him holler or say "bye" when he was finished calling.

I know the ground was soft, because we just had the most terrible rainstorm and flooding ever seen in Minnesota. Maybe, he didn't know the post was going to slant over or get yanked out by his horse. I did notice that particular day that he slowly got on his horse and trotted slowly away down the road. Hmmm...

Anyway, life goes on.

MY HEART DROPPED to HEAR the NEWS

It was the 7th of January and Thomas came over to the house to use the phone to call his horse training customers, as usual. I handed him his sticky note/phone bill showing the balance due of long distance calls he had made for a month.

"You can pay next time you come or whenever," I assured him. He has kept up in that regard.

"OK," he nodded.

After he got done, he caught my attention.

"I suppose you heard the news...?" I suppose you heard what happened to Sofie?...he paused again.

"No, I didn't," I responded with concern.

"She went missing a week ago last Saturday," Thomas continued.

My heart dropped when I heard this.

"Oh, no!" I exclaimed.

"Yes, yes, affirmed Thomas. You know, she went off to work for this guy. You know... with one of 'your people.'"

(I did not like it when I was referred to as 'your people.' It sounded degrading or tribal.)

"She never came home," he added.

...I thought for a moment. The last time I saw Sofie was when she came over to use the phone on Christmas eve to make a few calls. Before she left, I went upstairs to collect one big jar of a purple, mulberry scented candle and two smaller jars of red, scented candles to give to her for a Christmas present.

"Here's something for you!" I said, handing her a bag.

"I have something for you, too," she commented, thanking me for them.

"Oh, no. It is better to give than to receive," I said kindly.

"It is better to give than to receive," she agreed.

That was the last time I saw her.

Thomas continued to explain to me. My jaw was hanging open as I was still in awe...Somehow, I wasn't totally surprised. Sofie was the type to express time after time that she loved traveling and going to see places. After all, I remember, she once told me her birthday was on January 29th. She is going to be twenty-three years old soon.

Thomas continued, "We gathered some of us Amish together and went over to this guy's house to ask if he knew anything about Sofie or where she was?

This man said that he drove her somewhere and that Sofie said, 'I don't want to work for you anymore!' So, he left her there. He just lies, lies. Everyone knows he's that kind of guy. He has taken girls out of our community or helped them leave before. The county sheriff went out there and no one answered the door." We think she is with someone in another town."

"Your parents must be worried. Your mom must be hysterical," I said furiously.

"Oh, my mom is worried...but we're going to let it go for a while. Maybe, she will find out what it's like and come home."

Thomas excuses himself, "Well, I guess, I better go or my parents are going to think I'm missing. Well, thank you for letting me use the phone."

In a couple days, Thomas came over to use the phone again. He brought his younger brother Jess. This time, he told Ray and I that he was talking to the guy who Sofie worked for on the phone. He clarified with us when I asked him for "any news?" on her. Even though I had breakfast on the table, I was concerned to hear an update.

Thomas explained, "I didn't want to get him mad, so I acted like I didn't know that she was there. This way, he would tell me more. She is actually with this guy living in his house with his wife and family in the country. I heard a bunch of noise in the background. She is not with someone in another town like we thought. That was only from where she sent the letter to us saying that she was OK. This man took her shopping there and then the letter was mailed from that post office."

"As long as she isn't held against her will. Does she want to be there? I'd get the authorities to investigate the situation," I firmly suggested.

Thomas added, "Oh, she's in love, this guy said." He has a son who just broke up with another ex-Amish girl and likes Sofie now. He abused his older two children who are married now. He has two sons at home."

He politely thanked us and left back home with Jess.

My main concern as a neighbor and a friend is for Sofie's safety. Was this a decision she made on her own or was she swayed by this family that she is now with. If she went to work for this man who supposedly has a wife, why does he need Sofie to clean house. Was he just helping her out financially or what was his ultimate motive? Was it to have a mate for his son? Anyway, it remains to be seen.

WHO LET the COWS OUT?

Ray was driving us home from shopping in town, when we noticed two horse and buggies driven by Amish folks were crossing north one by one on the asphalt county road. There were about five more buggies waiting to cross, so we made our right turn north as well. They followed carefully one by one behind us. We waved as we passed each one and turned left after two fields toward our house. They were all most likely coming from church, since it was Sunday and about 2:15 PM.

Suddenly, I spotted what looked like a pack of wild dogs running loose on the gravel road in front of Thomas's parents, Alfred and Kitty's house. As we approached closer, it became clear.

"It looks like the cows broke out of their pen and are loose!" Ray clarified.

"Oh, I thought they were a bunch of dogs running wild," I muttered.

Ray drove a few yards past the Amish house, stopped, got out of the car, and shooed the seven or eight cows back toward the house. They all high tailed into the yard. As we turned right from the hill, getting closer to our house, it looked like most of the buggies were turning right after the two fields, not left toward Thomas's parents' house. I kept my head turned to eyeball their buggy to see if it turned in. It had to be one of two buggies, since the other buggy would be Richard's and his family that live across from Alfred.

About two, long minutes passed and we saw that a buggy went into

Alfred's yard. Alas! We could go home knowing they would notice and wonder how the cows got out or who let the cows out?

We would try to remember to mention it, when Thomas came around again to use the phone, pay his phone calls, or update us about Sofie…

It was early Monday afternoon, January 28th. Thomas came over to pay his phone bill and use the phone in the back porch. (Oh, I forgot to ask him about the cow escapade! I may remember next time.) I had an inkling that he was talking to the man where Sofie supposedly was when he asked to speak to his sister. I went to sit at my computer corner, so I wouldn't be listening to his conversation. When he got done, he stepped into the living room to let me know he was finished with his phone call.

"I'm all done with my call. I had to lie a little bit, you know, to find out stuff," he said.

I showed him our five newly born, almost one week old kittens of our new mother cat in the closet. He expressed that they looked really cute.

We walked back into the living room.

"Do you have any movies about sex?" Thomas asked inquisitively.

I was floored, figuratively, by that question! I instantly said, "Oh, I don't know, Thomas…"

I skipped the subject immediately.

"Oh, so, you were talking to that man who has Sofie," I asked.

"Yes."

"She isn't there. She is babysitting for someone. You know, your people," Thomas added. She's OK.

"Well, that's good. Sometimes, when we're that age, we need to find out who we are inside. We could have all the education in the world, but not know who we are as a person. We need to find out if something is good or bad for ourselves, I explained.

"Yeah, that's what my parents think. If she thinks she did something wrong, she may come back home, or if she thinks it was right, she will find that out, too. She is wearing regular clothes now. You know dressin' like you guys do, and wearing and letting her hair down," he continued.

Walking over to the kitchen table, I made sure Thomas got his change from his twenty dollar bill, paying for two months of phone calls, plus his portion of the service fee. I gave Ray the money. He was upstairs working "office in the home." He thanked me for letting him use the phone, said goodbye and left.

After Thomas left, I told Ray about Thomas's unbelievable question about wanting to see a movie about sex. He was about half amazed as I was. I, personally, couldn't believe my ears! (Remember, the Amish people have no access to the technology of movie theater. He, definitely, was not going to find or see any x-rated movies at our house.) I didn't even know if Thomas had a sweetheart, yet.

JUST WHEN THINGS WERE SETTLING DOWN... I THOUGHT

End of the third week in February, Thomas came over knocking loud enough for me to hear him as I was sitting down writing at the kitchen table. I went to open the door for him.

"Need to use the phone?" I asked.

"Yep! Yep!" he nodded.

I got the phone off the wall and handed it to him. I mentioned he could come in, if it was too cold in the back porch. He said that he was OK, proceeded to make his calls, and waited for a couple of calls back. During that time, he asked about the newly born kittens. They just turned 1 month. I showed him where they were in our laundry/washroom. All five kittens were playing in a made for human babies, old playpen that I bought for $5.00 from a local thrift shop. He was interested, as he has a bunch of cats running around his parents farm. His mother cat had a litter or two already. Anyway, the phone rang.

"It's probably for you..." I said. He picked up the phone off the wall and proceeded with his business/horse training calls.

When he got done, I asked him..."What's new?"

Oh, I don't know if you knew that my brother, Mickey...you know the one between Clay and Jess...was working with a saw

at the mill, and got his thumb chopped off.

"Oh, no...! I groaned. Gosh, da..! Excuse my French," I said.

"I know, I know..." Thomas acknowledged. By that time, Ray came into the kitchen from doing the taxes in the dining room, and showed concern.

"First, James, then Clay, then Theo...now Mickey, getting hurt," he reflected.

"I don't remember James getting hurt," I said.

"Oh," Thomas explained, "James got a finger sliced from a saw, too!"

"Before he was working with the crew on our addition, or after?" I questioned. curiously.

"That was after," he said.

I thought to myself, I recalled being told that Clay smashed his hip from an auger during corn harvest and Theo getting his finger tips sliced off from a saw used in carpentry. They both needed to go to the hospital in the city for treatment and follow up care. Now, it was Mickey and his thumb plus more hospital bills. I trust, the Amish community take care of their own in time of need.

"How's Sofie? I asked. Is she doing all right? Has she written lately? Is she making enough money? I wonder if she has to pay for her room and board?"

"Oh, she's doing Ok. No, she hasn't written anymore. I hope she is making a lot of money. I don't know if she pays anything where she stays," Thomas answered.

I added, "Well, as long as she is doing Ok.

"Well, I have to go now. Thanks for the phone," Thomas said, leaving to go home on his horse with a cart that was tied to one of the pine trees on the south side, front yard.

I, inquisitively, later asked Ray, "Couldn't they have grabbed Mickey's thumb, put it on ice, and taken it to the hospital to try to reattach it?"

Then I, instantly, thought...Amish do not keep ice.

Ray commented, "If they had put the piece of thumb in a snow filled cooler (It's winter! Naturally, there is snow and ice outside.) and taken it to the hospital, they could have disinfected it and reattached it, if it was a clean cut. That's wasn't done.

It is definitely a tough livelihood to be in construction. I would think there is someone to oversee these young apprentices until they are good to go on their own. I would only hope.

I, still, forgot to ask if he knew about the cows being out of the yard? Maybe, next time he's over here, I will.

TIME for SUNDAY MATINEE?

It was Sunday morning around 9:30 AM when Ray and I were getting ready to go into the city to eat at a restaurant and buy a few things. Guess who is knocking at the door? I could only guess that it was Thomas. I told Ray that someone was at the back door. I went to check and it was indeed Thomas and his next younger brother, Clay. After I opened the door, they stepped in. I immediately went to grab the wall landline phone to give to Thomas.

"Oh, we were just going out the door. We have to go somewhere. Could you make it quick with your calls? I asked assumingly. Oh, your customer, Jim Carson, called a few days ago and wants you to call him back. Could you make it in ten minutes, because we have to go."

"Oh, I don't think, I have his phone number," Thomas said, reaching into his inside pocket of his jacket.

Next thing I knew, he was talking to someone. Carson, perhaps. I always shut the kitchen door leading into the back porch room, so I really can't hear what is being said too clearly. It seems, he did have his phone number, but did they come over to use the phone? Was their intention to ask if they could watch a John Wayne movie or western? I gathered so, because after they left, I noticed that they didn't come over here with horse and buggy. They actually walked home slowly back down the road toward their house, so most likely they came on foot.

"Ray, I think they came over to see a movie... I said. Should I feel guilty?"

"No, no,' Ray affirmed. I don't think they cleaned up too good or changed their clothes. I could still smell their clothes. There was an animal or barn odor, he elaborated, understandably. Anyway, we have go."

We got in the car and headed down the road and passed the Amish boys.

"Maybe, we should have offered them a ride back to their house,' Ray told me. They just live down the hill. You know, their mom never knows where they go or how long they will be gone when they don't take the buggy. They just go walking."

I mentioned, "I imagine, they don't have church today, since they had time to come over."

"Oh, they will find something to do," Ray consoles.

(And yes, I forgot, again, to asked them about the cows out of the barn.)

Well, I did, finally, ask Thomas if he knew anything about the cows being out one Sunday? He came over to use the phone. After he made all his calls, I confronted him about the cow escapade.

"I meant to ask you if you knew your cows were out about a month and a half ago on Sunday," I asked.

Looking as if he was straining to think, "I don't remember anything. Someone could have let them out."

"Anyway, Roy had to stop and shew them back in the yard,' I explained. We figured that one of the six or seven buggies behind us on the road was yours or your family's and would turn in to see the cows in the yard. Was it church day?"

"Yes, it was. No, I don't recall anything," he said again.

I deducted, he was still at a church function or social, he was not coming home with his family in one of those buggies that day, or he just didn't want to admit to anything. He has been known to be evasive, like not admitting to the post out of the ground due to his horse yanking it out. Also, he hesitated for weeks to come and fix the fence, like he offered. I think, Sofie stirred him on to get it done since I tactfully told her about it. It's all a part of growing up and a little bit of wisdom.

Anyway, so life goes on.

A couple weeks later, when Thomas came over to call his horse training clients and let them know about their horses' progress, I heard him mention.

"I just thought, I'd let you know how everything is going, because I don't want to cheat you…"

I thought, how honorable a young man, he is.

After he got done with his calls, he told me that he was going to Wisconsin to sell some horses this weekend.

"I imagine you make a lot of money doing that?" I quizzed.

"Oh yeah, I do," he answered. He untied his horse from our tree and galloped back to his farm.

OH WHERE IS MY CAMERA?!

It was about 5:20 on a Friday evening. I started looking out my kitchen window as I usually do quite often. (Gazing into the south pasture helps me think about whatever comes to my mind first.) The neighbors who we rent the land to planted corn this year, but it, definitely, wasn't going to be "knee-high by the 4th of July!" This was because we had a late and cool spring this year. It was the first day of summer and the corn was rather less than mid shin high.

I saw and heard a loud, disturbing "clankety, clank, clank" noise on the road and it appeared that the Amish were slowly scraping the dirt. My first thought was Thomas, a horse trainer, was training a horse to work with a heavy machinery that cuts hay. Getting closer, I saw that it was Thomas and his four brothers following him by a couple of minutes with another noisy, old fashioned machinery, an old type of hay baler.

All of a sudden, I am seeing one of our emu birds walking back and forth along their fence, but mostly back toward the bird barn. My eyes told me it was outside of his fenced area in the south pasture where the corn was growing. I just had to go outside to confirm my suspicion that this emu was where he was. He was coming back, but out of his pen. I didn't know if he jumped out or the four other birds were also out. I had to call out for Ray right now.

I hollered in the north pasture where Ray was trimming trees.

"It looks like one of the emu birds is out! He is running the fence on this side. I'm sure, he is out of the fence!"

Sure enough, Ray went to take a look. I told him to go around this side of the sheep pen, because one of the big birds was coming toward it. He soon realized, all four emus ran out of their pasture into the corn field when the Amish came by on our side of the road.

"I'll tell them about their scaring the birds. I'll let them know!" I confidently told Ray.

At this time, Thomas had already gone past and made the left turn down the hill toward his house. His brothers were coming right along.

"Clankety, clank, clank..." I waved to stop them. Clay, the oldest of that group of brothers, stopped his horse and machinery and came up to me.

I exclaimed, "The emu birds got scared of the noise and ran away."

"Oh, I am sorry," Clay said. His brothers were all in awe."

"If you see any of the four missing birds, let us know."

"We sure will," responded Clay. They proceeded a few yards with their machine and stopped again.

Ray has approached to tell me, "The birds got scared of the noisy, old Amish machinery. They have metal wheels on their hay baler and that's makes a bunch of racket! This is a noise they are not used to hearing. They see and hear real well. Also, their little Jack Russell dog could have scared them since it was running along the machinery and in and out of half the yard when they went by. The birds want to go after any stray animal that enters their territory. Leave the gate open and stand by it so they don't go past the gate or further down the road. I'll take the car and go bring them back."

Okay, I had my orders.

Ray drove the car down past the south end of the corn field, parked it, climbed over the barb wire fence, slowly moved closer waving his arms, and allured the emus to bring them back. I was sure Ray knew how to handle these twelve year old birds, since he raised them since they were hatched here on the farm. Some long minutes went by before I saw Ray surfacing the slight curvature of the land's horizon.

Where is my camera?! I saw him walking, not running, but straddling an emu, guiding it toward the sheep pen and the house. He jumped on another emu from behind to, again, guide this 2nd one to face it in the right direction. I remember, Ray told me that one does not chase an emu, or he and the emu will be running forever.

Clay was standing with his brothers, observing how to bring in these birds. Ray was finally in the corner next to the bird pen. At this moment, I was wondered why Clay took off with his clanky machinery. I prayed that no bird went buzzerk again and darted in the opposite direction.

Ray ended up picking them up one by one and lifting them over the fence into the sheep pasture, in order to, ultimately, open the bird gate to get them to go in. I changed their water, gave them food, and gave them a hose shower. After he went to get the car, Ray sprayed all five down, as well. Emus love getting wet on a warm day.

Shortly after, we were standing by our garden when Thomas in the hay cutter came back to go further north down the road to widen the cut of the grass which was already mowed three feet toward the ditch by the county who cuts it about twice a year. A resourceful idea to collect the hay for their animals to feed on.

Next time we saw Thomas, we told him to warn us or let us know when they will be collecting the residual grass for hay on the sides of the road.

I asked him about how his sister Sofie was doing.

"She is okay and she is still taking care of children. She really likes children."

I continued, "Does she write her family?"

Thomas answered, "Oh, she wrote a note to my mom and dad for Mother's Day and Father's Day. She's all right."

"That's good," I added.

NICE DAY for a HAY RIDE

As I may have mentioned, every other Sunday the Amish went to church. Well, again, it was a Sunday that they stayed home and relaxed, or the kids go for a walk.

We both slept until about 8:00 that morning...up late the night before. I was in the living room sitting on the sofa.

A half an hour went by. All of a sudden, Ray had the kitchen door open and was talking to one of the Amish brothers. I saw the straw hat. This brother asked if they could watch TV. He was speaking on behalf of three of his other brothers.

"Oh, we haven't even had breakfast yet," I heard Ray answer.

It may have been Clay, because Ray, later, said that it wasn't Thomas. He wasn't sure which brother it was, but he was tall. He said that there were four boys that left and walked back home down the hill from us.

"I guess, they wanted to come over for their Sunday matinee," I told Ray. It's been a while.

A few hours later, I glanced out the window and saw that the boys were riding by, all sitting on a flat bed with hay for chairs. It, certainly, turned out to be a nice day for a hay ride!

NO MORE CALLS

He came over to use the phone one day during the summer to tell Ray and I that he will be renting the pasture from the people who live in the purple house next by his family's farm and house. He intended to train his horses there and use his neighbor's barn to house them as well. I thought one hundred fifty dollars a month was kind of steep! Ray did, too. That's five dollars a day. (Okay, it's easy math.)

At the end of July, Thomas came over in a horse and buggy and parked on our driveway, while I was in the garden.

Did you see me pass just now? He asked.

"I heard a buggy pass by, but I didn't know it was you,"

He was training one of his horses to buggy ride. Anyway, he came to tell me that he won't be using the phone anymore.

I asked assumingly, "So, you'll be using the phone there while you're working with the horses. It's all in one place and closer?"

"Yeah," Thomas assured me.

I said, that was great and it was okay.

He said, "I want to thank you for letting us use the phone all those times. I also want to thank you for when me and my brothers came over (to see TV). You were so nice to us.

"Oh, it was nothing!" I assured him.

"Oh, I intend to pay you for the phone. I'll be back again to pay you. I have a girl friend now. I'm going to Wisconsin for a few days to visit her."

"Is she a nice girl?"

"Oh, I think so…"

"Just like I told your brother James and Sofie… take your time. Don't rush things. You will know if it is the right person for you," I professed.

"Okay, thanks. Anyway, I'll be back to pay you for the phone."

"Say hi, to your mom for me," I called.

"Okay," Thomas called back.

He directed the horse to go down the drive and turn around. He was off, going back on the county road, and down the hill to his parent's home.

Sure enough, he came back on August 1st to pay us the balance which was twenty-one dollars and sixty cents. He handed me thirty dollars and said to keep the change.

"Oh, no…no," I exclaimed.

Thomas insisted for us to keep the change. I gave the cash to Ray, since he pays the phone bill. Actually, that took care of his part of the monthly service charge. Ray was already informed by me that Thomas chose not to be using our phone since he will be renting the pasture from the couple close by his folks farm.

"WE DON'T NEED ANY MEAT"

One of our older ewe's was going crippled for the last four years. We needed to put her down soon. Ray thought it would be a good idea and wonderful gesture to ask the Amish if they would be needing some meat. He decided to drive down and ask Richard, another Amish neighbor, if he'd be interested in our sheep. He was still at work on Saturday. Ray told me that his wife said to best catch him before 8:00 AM to talk to him, but didn't think they needed any meat. She said to ask Thomas's family across from them.

Ray also asked her about possibly buying some eggs from them. Richard's wife mentioned that all their eggs from their chicken farm are contracted to a distributor. They only eat the cracked ones.

Ray went to ask Thomas's family. Ray said that he approached their house and Thomas came out to greet him. I guess, he saw Ray coming. He asked him if he could use some lamb meat. Thomas went in the house to ask his mom and dad and came back out saying, "No, we can't use any meat."

"Do you know of any farm that has sheep, so I may get a ram for my ewes?" Ray continued.

"You might ask the farm past the county road two or three farms down that have some sheep. They may have one."

Ray came back home to tell me all about it. They didn't want to take our elder ewe off our hands. We just concluded that they had enough beef, lamb, and chicken meat for their families to last them forever.

I know that they preserved their meat with salt once an animal was slaughtered. All I can think of is so much for high blood pressure. The Amish community truly took take of their own in every way, shape, or form, if need be.

"I think they are too proud, Ray. Don't worry about it," I commented.

Ray responded, "I won't bother them when they go to church every other Sunday. Besides, they don't work on Sunday. I still need to talk to Richard about other stuff like residing the big barn."

THE DAY WE SAW HER AGAIN

I believe that the friends that we make, people that we meet or help will return to see us again to touch our lives. The day we saw her (Sofie) again was

December 27th, less that a month before she turned twenty-four years old. I remembered her birthday, as she once told me.

"There's a red van coming up the driveway and is parking, I shouted to Ray, as I was looking out the window. Come take a look."

He looked out the porch window, at the van and went to open the back door. In walked a medium height, strong built young lady with a brown pony tail, black jacket over a white blouse, and jeans and black, contemporary boots.

"Hi," Sofie said softly.

"Oh, I didn't recognize you, Sofie!" I said, in amazement.

Roy also said the same thing!

How are you!?" I asked inquisitively.

"I am good," she responds.

Ray and I asked Sofie to come into the kitchen.

"You are so pretty and you look good…Are you wearing any make up? Not a lot…huh? I continued.

"Yes, I am. Just a little," she answered.

"Your eyes look nice. The're glowing," Do you visit your family?" I asked.

She said, "I don't talk to my mother or brothers. They don't speak to the "English" (outsiders). "I went to visit my uncle about twenty-five miles west of here. When I left, I left. I had enough. I drove by the house and they just stared," she explained.

I mentioned, "I saw your brothers, Thomas and Theo at the food center in town. I asked them how is everything? They told me, 'Oh, fine, just fine.'"

"You got a car? Is that your car outside?" I asked.

"No, I borrowed this car. I do have a car now, but it's not four wheel drive. The roads are icy and I need four wheel drive. I got my license now, but it took me a long time to get my permit though," I tried to call and leave a message, Sofie continued.

"Oh, I couldn't understand what you needed, since you spoke a few words, something about "get my brothers…?" Was it an emergency?" I pried.

"Oh, no, it wasn't. If it was, I'd say it was."

I told her, "Yes, if it's an emergency, tell us."

"He still rents the pasture across to train his horses, doesn't he?" Ray asked.

"Oh, he doesn't rent anymore," she confirmed. He doesn't have a girl friend anymore."

(Perhaps, Sofie talked to him by phone earlier.)

"Gosh, for one hundred fifty dollars a month to rent that pasture, they ought to let him use the phone, too,' I added. Thomas stopped using our phone some time ago this year."

Sofie said, "Thomas is of age now. He can use the community phone down the road."

"So what are you doing now?" I asked.

"You mean, for work?' she replied… 'I've been working in the kitchen at a nursing home washing dishes and cleaning houses. I will be going into training as a cook for the nursing home soon."

"Wow, that's so great! Now, you're getting real money, a check regularly."

We both praised her.

I went to get a red, cinnamon candle and handed it to her.

"I gave you a candle a year, before I last saw you, before Christmas last year. I'll give you another one when I see you again.

She smiled.

"So, are you getting married?" I asked, with concern.

"Oh no, I am too shy with people. I am not ready yet."

"Don't worry… you'll meet someone special someday and you'll know it when the time comes," I assured her.

Ray and I each gave her a big hug and a hug again right before she had to get going. It was so great to see her again.

She turned the van around and drove down the road, turning left toward her parent's house, perhaps to see it one more time…

What a nice, little visit. She is now a grown, independent, and happy woman still developing her confidence and personality at almost twenty-four years old. She feels good and is okay within herself about her decision to leave the community that she was reared in. As I always respected her way of life, I never once told her to leave. Ray and I only wondered in our minds if she would ever make that step. I thought about her several times this year hoping that she was doing fine wherever she was staying. I can come away from this whole experience of being a friend to the Amish, feeling good that I was there to help in a time of need. I know, I will see her again someday…

UPDATE:

End of April of 2009, I met Theo at the local food center in town. I was shopping in the meat department when he called my name. I turned to recognize him. He came up to me to tell me that he was going to have some one drive him to North Carolina to get an operation for a hernia in the groin area. I thought, why so far? Apparently, he had been doing heavy lifting. I wished him well and asked how long he was going to be there. I figured a week or so. That's what he thought as well. I asked him if that was him riding the buggy into town. He acknowledged that it was him. I passed him going home crunching over and we waved to each other. That hernia must have been hurting him all right.

One Sunday afternoon, Ray and I were driving home the back way from shopping. We were approaching Thomas's house and saw a horse on the loose out of the corral on the road. We decided to pull in to let the family know. I knocked at the door and there were his parents, Alfred & Kitty, at the door. I asked if Thomas was around so I could tell him that a horse was out. Alfred told us he'd let Thomas know. I also wished Kitty a "Happy Mother's Day." She grinned so gently and said "Thank you."

It was mid June and Clay was knocking at the kitchen door. He asked to use the phone so I said okay. I am thinking nothing of it even though he talked on it for about twenty-five minutes. He said, he'd pay when I told him that Ray sizes up the phone statement and we'd let him know.

The next day, about 8:00 PM, Sofie came knocking. I was surprised to see her again. She told me that Clay called her because he wants to leave the Amish community. He can't use the community phone until he turns twenty-one years old. That made sense of why Thomas stopped using our phone a year or so ago.

Sofie now has a metallic, tan pickup truck with a rusted wheel well. I told her… as long as the engine is in good, running condition… She wants to get a better vehicle. She is still working (cooking) for the nursing home, works at a Mexican restaurant, and cleans houses. She is saving her money, however, she does party socially with other girls and guys. I told her to be very careful. She nodded.

I made a point of telling Sofie that I had my response ready for her parents if they ever came over to ask me if I had anything to do with her leaving the Amish. She knew, I didn't influence her decision, as I told her she that she had a 'mind of her own.' I only tried to guide and give her emotional support. She was aware of that.

She agreed, "I definitely have a mind of my own. I always have and always will."

Lastly, Sofie said, "If Clay comes around, tell him to call me. If he wants to leave, the best time to escape is at night. He could find a job…"

I asked her if she will stop by her parents or friends down the way?

She answered, "I could, but I won't, I won't…' I'll drive up and down, by the house on my way home."

I wished her well and she drove off.

THE CULTURE of the AMISH

In conclusion, as much as I truly believe the Amish people will someday have use of technology and its gadgets, I do know they are struggling without it today. For one thing, from time to time they need to go to a neighbor to use a phone for calling customers or clients outside their community, of course. For another thing, they have absolute no electricity in their house. They do use power tools in construction, although they did when they worked on our home. They use kerosene lamps in their homes, hand pumped water in the kitchen, and wood burning stoves.

Amish Faith -

The old order of Amish and Mennonites or the "Plain people" commit themselves to a life of pacifism and nonviolence. They will not use force in the event they are attacked by someone, because of their commitment to God. They are Christians, therefore they believe in Jesus Christ as their savior. They take the Bible word for word. For example, they are against having their pictures taken. They quote Exodus in the Bible, and stand by the 2nd amendment.

There is the Ordnung or what old order Amish call the "ordinance or discipline." It is the "understood behavior" by which Amish are supposed to live and is taught early on to Amish youth. Some Amish have been torn between tradition and change. Certain details of the Ordnung are different between church districts and settlements. For example, smoking and drinking is predominately banned throughout the Amish communities, but I have heard that a few communities allow pipe smoking or chewing tobacco.

The Amish are a community of people dedicated to a simpler, family centered way of life. They practice humility and separation from the world. A part of this faith is exemplified by the way they dress.

Amish Dress -

Amish women and girls wear modest, solid colored dresses with long sleeves and a full skirt that is mid shin, below the calf, or floor length. They wear capes and aprons over their dresses fastened with straight pins or snaps. They tie their hair in a bun on the back of their head, since they do not cut their hair. A white prayer cap is worn if females are single and a black one, if they are married. Absolutely, no jewelry is adorned.

Men and boys wear dark-colored - fastened with hooks and eyes - suits and vests, no lapel coats, trousers, suspenders, solid-colored - buttoned shirts - mostly aqua, green, that I've seen, and black socks and shoes. Black or straw broad brimmed hats are worn. Once Amish men marry, they will grow a beard and they do not have mustaches.

An Amish community and family will shun a member who has broken the set rules of the church or his baptismal vows. It is hard to not sit at the same table with a shunned member of the family, as their family get-togethers could be uncomfortable. They do not pass judgment on the rest of society or outsiders.

School -

The Amish children's first language before going to school is Dutch which is taught at home. I learned this when Sofie brought her youngest brother, Larry, to our house. I realized that he did not understand me two years ago. Children learn English when they start school. Children go to school from 1ˢᵗ to 8ᵗʰ grade. It is a one room school house in which there are individual desks for eight to fifteen children for each area of Amish farms. The most beautiful thing is the song that they sing thanking God before they leave school each day. I noticed this when I was asked by the general store owner to pick up her little daughter. They, then, go to work at a craft and learn from the adults.

Courting & Marriage -

Once they are sixteen years old, they can look for someone they might want to marry. The young women have to be twenty and the young men have to be in their twenty's, as well as a member of the church, in order for them to marry.

Medical -

Families have their own funds, but rely on financial support from fellow Amish and the community church, if an emergency arises, especially when they need to go to the hospital to be treated. They do go to local doctors in town as I have seen women in the doctor's office. If someone has a certain ailment, members may travel a bit of a distance to see a specialist recognized by their community.

Dental -

They go to a dental specialist to get dentures. Speaking first hand, when I took Sofie to the local "general dentist" (her relative) in the area... He takes care of tooth pullings.

Husband or sons' occupations -

Amish livelihoods are woodworking in furniture and cabinetry, training horses, constructing houses and barns, farming corn, baling hay, tending to livestock (cows, work horses, chickens, pigs, and goats), managing a general store (although a wife could manage store), and designing wrought iron for fencing and buggies, etc.

Housewife and daughters' duties -

Female duties/chores were canning tomatoes, applesauce, berries, etc., baking bread, pies, cookies, rolls and cooking meals from a wood burning stove, washing clothes by hand and hanging them to dry on a clothesline on Fridays, house cleaning, gardening, raking, sewing clothes, ironing, teaching, caring for children, being a midwife, weaving baskets (although men wove hats, I believe), and making quilts, pillows, and aprons, etc.

If I didn't mention it, I made a flyer for Kitty to advertise her quilts and crafts store in her home. I hung a copy at the food center's community bulletin board in town and gave her some copies to boot. It said, "Please come visit us! Amish homemade: woven baskets, colorful quilts, quilted pillows, quilted kitchen towels, pot holders, close pen holders, etc. I described directions to get to her house with address tickets to pull from the bottom of the flyer. That was the least I could do. I didn't charge her. After about five years, she gave up her store. That room was transformed into a bakery where Sofie baked her fresh pies, cookies, bread, and rolls to sell at the park. Remember, she asked me to make her some signs. I made two cardboard signs and a few poster-flyers for her, as well. Sofie never paid me for the signs, so I considered it a good deed on my part. Besides, I was happy to help her in some way.

I only wonder if and when they will ever resort to electricity and/ or automobiles and not keep relying on kerosene lamps, candles, horse drawn buggies, and primitive farm equipment? Again, this is their way of life. I, truly, respect that.

LaVergne, TN USA
10 August 2010
192832LV00002B/1/P